The Worst Thing She Ever Did

Also by
Alice Kuipers

Life on the Refrigerator Door

Alice Kuipers

The Worst
Thing She
Ever Did

Harper_Trophy_**Canada**™
An imprint of HarperCollins*Publishers*Ltd

Published by Harper*Trophy*Canada™,
an imprint of HarperCollins Publishers Ltd.

First published by Harper*Trophy*Canada™
in an original trade paperback edition: 2010
This Harper*Trophy*Canada™ paperback edition: 2013

HarperCollins books may be purchased for educational, business,
or sales promotional use through our Special Markets Department.

HarperCollins Publishers Ltd
2 Bloor Steet East, 20th Floor
Toronto, Ontario, Canada
M4W 1A8

The author gratefully acknowledges the lines from "i have found what you
are like." Copyright 1923, 1925, 1951, 1953, © 1991 by the Trustees for
the E. E. Cummings Trust. Copyright © 1976 by George James Firmage,
from *Complete Poems: 1904–1962 by E. E. Cummings*, edited by George J.
Firmage. Used by permission of Liveright Publishing Corporation.

www.harpercollins.ca

Library and Archives Canada Cataloguing in Publication
information is available upon request

ISBN 978-1-55468-021-4

Printed and bound in the United States
RRD 10 9 8 7 6 5 4 3 2 1

To my brother, his wife, and their daughter

And then the windows failed, and then
I could not see to see.

—*Emily Dickinson*

The Worst

Thing She

Ever Did

1

The sticks on the trees
Stand up harsh and bare

SUNDAY, JANUARY 1ST

I look at the words, black like inky spiders, and watch
the webs they weave. There's something enjoyable about
filling a blank page, although I'd never admit that to Lynda.
She gave me this empty notebook when I went to see her
on Thursday and said, "Writing in here will help you
remember."

"What if I don't want to?"

"I think you should."

"It won't change anything."

"Perhaps you need to try this."

I rolled my eyes.

She said in her terribly patient way, "Do you want to talk about what you're feeling right now?"

"I'm fine," I said, wishing the hour were over.

TUESDAY, JANUARY 3RD

I wonder what to write. I don't even know where to start, but I do like the act of writing. I suppose I could start with this morning.

After a horrible dream I woke tired. Most people I know would be dreading going back to school, but I was glad to get out of the house. Today was the first day back to St. David's High after our Christmas holiday. It's ten minutes' dreary walk and seven stops on the bus from my house in Islington, North London. It's a girls' school. I'm in my first year of sixth form, but because my birthday's in July, I won't be seventeen for ages.

I stood in my bra, knickers, and tights and tugged on my uniform. I buttoned the pale blue shirt (small), zipped up my navy skirt (medium), and rolled it at the waist to make it about two inches shorter. I tugged on my navy jumper and wrestled into my blazer, with its horrible shoulder pads, smoothing down the front lapels next to the insignia with the words *Nil Ye Dread*. I slipped on black ballet flats.

Where my tongue dips toward my throat, I had a bitter, burned coffee taste, which even brushing my teeth couldn't remove. Was I nervous?

I picked up the brown bag Emily got me from Leeds, hurried along the corridor, passing Emily's room, Mum's office, and clattering down the wooden stairs into the kitchen. Mum (she's an interior designer—at least she used to be) chose the white walls and hardwood floors that we have in every room except the kitchen, which has red cork tile. The round oak table had no one sitting at it. Knowing there was no bread or milk, I didn't bother stopping for breakfast. I called upstairs to Mum, "I'll be back later." She didn't answer. I wasn't even sure she was up there.

I went through the living room, past the shelves of books and the cool photographs that Emily took of plastic bags. I opened the front door and walked out into the chilly morning. The clouds were drenched with grey light like thick smoke. I tried not to think about anything, tried to empty my mind, but I couldn't help it, and for a moment the memories were too strong. I held out one trembling hand like I was an old woman with Parkinson's and watched it shake. My lungs were filling with smoky clouds; the air was too thick to breathe. I leaned against a neighbor's fence. Took deep breaths. Reminded myself that everything was fine.

I got on the bus, concentrated on looking out the window, and arrived at St. David's in one piece. As I walked

3

under the stone arch to the main building, I kept telling myself I was okay; it was time I got over last summer. The autumn term passed by in a fog, but now it's a new year, new term, new start—for real this time. I ducked past reception, waved to a couple of people, avoided answering any questions about Christmas, avoided looking at their silly bright smiles. I pushed down the corridor, squeezed past the crush of other girls walking arm in arm, speaking on their mobiles, being yelled at by Mrs. P to slow down.

Everything going on around me—the others, the noise, the ring of the bell to get to class—was so loud, it gave me a headache. The strip lights along the ceiling fizzed neon yellow, the color too bright for my eyes. I took a slow breath. I remembered my New Year's resolution: I'm moving on from everything that's happened. I'm not going to talk about it, think about it, let the memory pounce upon me like a waiting tiger, nothing.

I got to my form room and looked around for my best friend, Abigail, but she wasn't sitting at her seat at the desk by the window, the one close to the maps of the world that Ms. Bloxam insists on. Abi was late. Or I was early. I remember how Abi and I used to meet at the school gate and chat about the morning and the night before even though we'd have spent all evening on the phone or IM together. Abi and I met on the very first day of school years ago, standing in the corridor waiting nervously to

4

go into our first lesson. She came over and said hi, and I thought she was brave to do that, because I was too shy to go up to anyone. We quickly became close. We went through everything together. I was the calm, strong, supportive one, good at school, good at listening; she was fun, impulsive, lively. She made me laugh.

I sighed and went to sit down. A new girl sat at the desk next to mine. She made our uniform look good. (I thought it wasn't possible.) Her shirt was not too tight or too loose and the color suited her milky skin. Her short skirt showed the fishnet pattern in her black tights and her shoes had a small heel.

She sat, leaning over the desk, writing something, her crow-feather hair falling all over the place, long and shiny. Without looking up, she said, "Are you going to keep staring at me or are you going to say something?"

I didn't reply. She looked up then and narrowed her denim blue eyes. She said, "What?"

"Nothing. I just . . . It's just that Megan sits there."

"Well, Megan's gonna have to sit somewhere else today."

I'd never think to say anything obvious like that. I'm all apologies and flubbed words when people confront me. Which isn't often anymore. I wasn't sure how to reply. "Are you American?" I asked.

She folded the paper she'd been writing on and pushed

5

her hair back from her face. "I'm from Canada. But I live here now."

"How come?"

"My mom died and I moved here two weeks ago to live with my dad." She paused. "What?" she said, again.

"I'm sorry about your mum."

She shrugged and said, "Not your fault." Leaning back in her chair, she made the front two feet come off the floor.

"What were you writing?" I asked.

"Nothing."

"I'm just curious."

"A poem."

"What sort of a poem?" I'd never met anyone who wrote poems.

"A poem about death."

I couldn't tell if she was being serious. It wasn't the sort of thing I'd joke about. "You're going to be in our class?" I asked.

"What do you think?" She reached into her pocket and pulled out a packet of chewing gum. She offered me some with a quick smile, but I shook my head.

The bell rang and some of the others came into the classroom. The new girl stayed exactly where she was. The others looked at her like she was an animal at the zoo they couldn't quite believe in—like an okapi or a red panda. Abigail came over and gave me a big squealing hug.

6

"Where were you all Christmas, Sophie? How've you been?"

She was only being nice, but I couldn't help but tense up, because everything has just been so weird between us. I immediately mentally kicked myself for being ridiculous; I wanted to start the new term with everything NORMAL. Abi looked at the new girl but didn't speak to her, not even to say hi or anything. She—Abi, not the new girl—put her hand on my shoulder and talked to me about some party she wanted to have at her house. I half listened to Abi and half watched the Canadian, who unfolded her piece of paper, chewed her pen, then went back to writing her poem.

The second bell rang. Ms. Bloxam came in. She's so enormous and unfit that I suspect she'll have a heart attack one of these days. I imagine her taking registration with sweat beading at the edges of her puffy face. Suddenly, between reading out "Sophie Baxter" (me) and "Megan Bigley," she'll make this strangled sound, clutch her heart, slump over her desk, and writhe about gasping for breath, but it'll be too late. She'll die in front of us all, never finishing registration.

Today, though, she finished registration, not mentioning the new girl or seeming to notice when Megan arrived late and perched on a spare seat with her arms folded across her chest, glaring at everyone. Ms. Bloxam asked if we'd had a nice Christmas and rambled, "It's a new term and we're all looking forward to . . . er . . . moving on from the . . . er . . . terrible events of last year. You girls, all of you"—I'm sure she gave me a look—"have to start focusing on all we have to learn, on all"—she took a breath at this point because she'd run out of air—"on all that is coming to you, with all the rigor . . . er . . . necessary for you to approach your future. Before you know it, you'll be in the thick of . . ."

I tuned out. Stuck my pen into the wood of the desk, wrote the first letter of my name. S. Sophie. I wondered if I had a brand-new name I would be a brand-new person. A person without a past. A person with only the future as remains. I carved the S harder into the wood and felt heat at my back. I spun around, but there was nothing there. No heat, no nothing. Just Zara painting her nails with a silver star at the tip of each manicured finger. Zara's black, and she has her hair cropped pixielike around her ears. She looks like a model. Zara pouted at me: her way of smiling. I turned around to face the front again. Ms. Bloxam, still sweating and still rambling on, told us we're having a dance teacher come in from Manchester in a couple of weeks. Then, finally, she introduced us to the new girl. Her name's Rosa-Leigh. Megan jumped up, interrupted, and said Rosa-Leigh was in her seat.

Megan's short with big boobs. Her hair is wiry and plain, muddy brown. She has a large mouth with annoyingly

8

perfect teeth. She uses fake tan to make herself less pale. Her eyes are hazel, which makes them sound pretty, but I find they're too yellow with her fair skin; even when she has on loads of fake tan, her eyes just seem the wrong color. I've never liked her. I think of her as doughy, like an uncooked bread roll, maybe because she's a bit shapeless, apart from her big boobs, but that's really mean of me to think—I'm hardly perfect when it comes to body shape. I suppose I don't like her because she's a "hanger-on." She's always *there*. You'd think it might be because she's insecure or something, but it's not that, because she *loves* herself. Ms. Bloxam pressed her lips together, looked at Megan, then swiveled around, and told Rosa-Leigh to move to a spare desk on the left.

I watched Rosa-Leigh. As did the rest of the class: thirty pairs of eyes. She waited for just long enough that everyone thought she wasn't going to move; then, at the last second, she picked up her things, stood, said, "Sure," and shifted.

The first lesson I had was double Art. Then break. Then English and History. At lunch Abigail grabbed me and propelled me to the table with her and Megan. Zara came to sit with us, and I listened while the three of them gabbled on about homework, and Megan's boyfriend, and Zara's great Christmas in Spain. I didn't say much. Everything changed last term, so now we all sit together and I have to pretend Abigail and I didn't used to laugh at how Megan

9

and Zara are boring and shallow. I still don't like Megan, or even Zara, really, and Abigail didn't used to, either. Abi told me last year that she didn't trust Megan and that Zara made her feel small and stupid. That doesn't seem to be the case anymore. So I sat there being normal and laughing in all the right places, because that's how things are now.

They started talking about Abigail's party. (She's throwing it because her mum's away the weekend after next.) Megan's getting to Abigail's house at five and everyone else can come over at eight. Everyone else being me, as well. It used to be I was the one to get there early. I remember once, years ago, Abi and I had planned a huge sleepover at her house. We were so excited as we spent the afternoon before everyone arrived, choosing movies and piling up packets of crisps and chocolates for our midnight feast. It got to eight o'clock, and no one showed up. She was ready to cry, so we stuffed ourselves with crisps and watched half the movies before we realized we'd told everyone the wrong day. They all showed up the next evening, and Abi and I were exhausted from having stayed up all the night before. For years we made jokes about our lack of "organizing sleepover" skills until only one of us had to say the word *sleepover* for the other to crack a smile. I wondered if Abigail remembered, too. I glanced over at her, but she wasn't looking at me. She was busy going on about how "Megan has her brother's friends coming, and Megan has a great idea for the music." I couldn't wait to get out of the packed lunch hall.

SATURDAY, JANUARY 7TH

Tonight Mum ordered us Chinese takeaway for dinner: lemon chicken, sweet and sour pork, egg fried rice. We picked at our food in silence. Straight after she'd finished, she left the table and spent the rest of the evening in her office with her collection. I went out to buy poor Fluffy some cat food and fed her as soon as I got back. She purred and rubbed around my legs in gratitude. I switched on the kettle. I was going to ask Mum if she wanted a hot drink, but when I went upstairs, through the door I could hear her crying. I hurried down and made myself a lonely cup of tea (no milk, yuck). I switched on the computer so when Mum came out I looked busy and she didn't know I'd heard.

MONDAY, JANUARY 9TH

Rosa-Leigh, the new girl, and I catch the same bus home, but she never speaks to me. Instead she heads upstairs as soon as we get on. I'm glad. I get to spend the journey looking out the window, not thinking about anything.

TUESDAY, JANUARY 10TH

Tonight I did all my homework and watched the telly for a couple of hours. There's never anything on except for home makeovers or really violent stuff that I can't watch. I switched it off and sat for a while. In the gloom of evening, I wished Abigail would call. We're best friends, after all. I know it's because she doesn't know what to say, she even told me that, but I wished she'd call anyway.

Abigail called, just this minute. Weird. I told her I was writing and she wanted to know what I was writing about. I told her it was private. There was an awkward pause, even though we'd been on the phone only ten seconds, then she switched topics. She said that Megan is asking her brother and all his friends to her party, which she'd already said at lunch the other day, and that one of his friends plays in a club somewhere nearby—in Camden. I had a pain go through me at the thought that Megan was planning the party with her—Megan is around all the time now.

Abigail said, "What's wrong?"

"Nothing."

"Do you want to, you know, come over?"

I thought about walking to the station, buying a ticket, getting over to her house, like I've done a thousand times before. My head began to hurt. "I've got homework."

"You haven't finished it already?" I knew she meant, *That's not like you.* "Come on, Soph, come over. We can hang out."

"No," I said. "I've gotta go." The words came out shorter than I wanted, but once they were said I couldn't unsay them. I know she's only trying to be nice, to be normal like I want, but it's like I can't stop myself. I don't understand why I can't just be NORMAL. Everything's fine. I'm fine, but I keep being WEIRD. I NEED TO MOVE ON. "Bye," I said.

I put the phone down and then worried for ages that she would be mad or hurt or whatever, but when I called her back to say sorry, her mobile was switched off. I rang her landline and her mum answered. She has a thick accent from her native Russia. She left when she married Abi's dad and moved to the UK, which she's always hated. Abi's dad left her when Abi was eight, and it was too late for her to go back. She told me that Abigail had gone to Zara's with Megan. I imagined Abi, Zara, and Megan all hanging out together.

Abigail's mum said, "How are *you* doing?"

"I'm fine. How are you?" I wish people would stop asking.

"Everything's great here. Except, now I've got you on the phone, Sophie, do you think Abigail's all right?"

"She seems fine."

"And *you*? How are *you*?"

"Really, I'm fine." I cringed. I just want to be asked to go and hang out at stupid Zara's. "Yeah, fine," I said. "See you soon, Mrs. Bykov."

WEDNESDAY, JANUARY 11TH

When I got to school today, Abigail was waiting by the stone arch. She waved her skinny arm over her head. "Hey!" she yelled. She has these wild red curls, and because it was

13

drizzling, they were even frizzier than normal. She must have seen me looking at her hair, because she smoothed it down as I came over and said, "I know, stupid rain."

"It looks fine," I lied. She tucked her arm through mine as we walked into school. I could smell cigarette smoke on her uniform.

"What have you been up to?" she said.

"Not much."

"How's everything going?"

"Good." I pulled at my brain for something to say. Why was it that talking to my best friend suddenly felt like talking to some stranger who comes up to me in the street trying to get me to give money to some charity? What was WRONG with me? Finally I came up with "How are things going with the party?"

"Great. You can come over early with Megan if you like. Come at five." She paused. "Only if you want."

I felt a flutter of pleasure. Things were going to be all right. "Sure," I said. "Okay."

"Some of Megan's brother's friends are really cute. There's this one guy who I can't stop thinking about. He's tall with AMAZING blue eyes. . . ." She trailed off. "So, it's good to see you doing so much better. I thought last term you might never, you know, recover."

"Yeah," I said. We were in the corridor leading to the classroom. The crush of girls was making me sweat. I imagined that if more and more people crowded into the corridor

14

it could turn into one of those tramplings at concerts you read about. A drip of perspiration started working its way down my shirt. I pulled at my collar with my free hand. "Yeah, I'm doing really well."

She squeezed my arm hard. "Good," she said. "I've missed you."

"Yeah." This was what I'd wanted her to say, so why couldn't I just catch my breath and concentrate on the moment?

"You know you're my best friend, right?"

A girl pushed past me, jolting my shoulder. In my mind the crush got worse and girls started screaming like they were being murdered. Real terror licked along my spine with a flame tongue. I stammered, "I've just remembered . . . I've left something up in the art room."

"I'll go with you."

"No, you'll end up being late." I activated the muscles in my face to make a smile happen, like a clockwork cuckoo.

Abi's eyes narrowed, but I was already heading away from her.

I had to get out of there. "See you later!" I yelled, and pushed my way through the tangled limbs of the crowded space, fighting my way for air. I got out through a side door.

In the fresh air I felt calmer, and I wondered what I was going to do with myself. I didn't need to go to the art room at all. It was too late to go back to find Abigail and apologize for being so insane. I went and stood on the tarmac overlooking the playing field. It's a raggedy bit of grass streaked with mud where girls have torn it up during hockey and track. My eyelashes moistened in the drizzle. It was just another grey day. That's all I had to remember.

THURSDAY, JANUARY 12ᵀᴴ

I just want to forget. When I said this to stupid "Ms. Brown Please Call Me Lynda"—who is round and soft and who looks at me with eyes like a hurt kitten when I don't want to talk to her—she replied gently, "Do you really think so? I'm not sure burying it all inside is going to help."

She was so wrong, it made me want to scream. Instead I decided not to speak for the whole hour. I got so bored, I felt like my tongue might fall out of my mouth like a slug out of a lettuce. I had to keep my eyes open because if I closed them I could see Emily, which is the last thing I want, but keeping my eyes open meant I could see the sympathy and patience on Lynda's face.

I got so sick of it, I leaped up and stormed out, slamming the door. Lynda's place of work is an ordinary terraced house, brick, two floors. The curtains are yellow, a happy color, hospital cheer. I turned away and marched down the road.

I heard Lynda yell after me, so I ducked into a corner shop. I wandered up and down the aisles, then went to

16

the counter and looked at the cigarettes. I wanted to buy a packet, although I don't even smoke. I put my hands in my pockets, looking with my fingers for money, but I didn't have any. The scrawny man behind the counter noticed me and frowned. Abigail and Megan smoke; Zara and I don't. I wondered for about two seconds if things with Abigail would go back to normal if I took it up, but that was just me being stupid.

He said, "Can I help you?"

I didn't answer. I just got the hell out of his shop.

2

With rings on their fingers
And knots in their hair

FRIDAY, JANUARY 13ᵀᴴ

It's Abigail's party tonight. At least Mum's giving me a ride so I don't have to get the train.

I don't know what to wear. I called Abigail to ask what she thought, but her phone was busy. Megan's phone was busy, too. I sat on the bed for ages trying not to be annoyed that they were obviously talking to each other. I'm so pathetic.

In the end I called Megan again, but this time she

answered. Of course I didn't have anything to say because I'd only called to see if she was still speaking to Abigail, and all I could come up with to ask was what she thought I should wear to the party. I heard in her voice that she thought I was being ridiculous, but she said, "I'm wearing a skirt and top I bought last weekend with Abi."

I don't like wearing skirts. I'll wear my jeans instead.

SATURDAY, JANUARY 14TH

It's really late and I just got back from the party. I'm glad I wore jeans. Megan was wearing jeans and so was everyone else. I'd have looked totally stupid in a skirt.

I slept badly. I had a horrible dream about being stuck in a well that was filling with water so I couldn't get out, then the dream changed and I dreamed about the party. When I woke, I couldn't remember for a while what had really happened and what was nightmare. I'm so sick of bad dreams, I feel like giving up sleeping.

So, I got to Abigail's late because I took so long deciding what to wear. Megan and Abi were putting on makeup in Abi's room. I love her room; I've stayed there thousands of times. I love the tangerine walls and the red and yellow floral bedcover from Mexico and the wooden planks balanced on bricks to make shelves alongside the bed. Above the shelves is a huge batik of the sun and the ocean. Her brother got it for her from Indonesia. It's not the sort of thing Abi usually likes nowadays—too flaky for her; she's more into things that are fashionable—but I think it makes her whole room feel like sunrise.

Abi sat cross-legged on the bed, hunched over her sister's mirror. She put concealer under her eyes and said, "I hate my stupid sister." Then she looked at me, her mouth open, the words hanging between us. She added really fast, "I mean, she's so annoying. She screamed at me for taking the mirror. Thank God she's only back from university for a few more days."

I didn't know what to say so I looked through her wardrobe.

She said, "Why don't you borrow my white shirt?"

I was glad the subject was changed. "Sure," I said, because the shirt makes me look like I've got bigger boobs.

Then she threw me over a pair of trousers. "They don't fit me anymore, and you're definitely thinner than me now."

Megan didn't say anything. It was almost like she wasn't in the room.

Abigail said gently, "How's your mum?"

I shrugged. "Not good. She spends all her time with her collection."

Then I wished I hadn't spoken because Megan said in her nasal voice, "What collection?"

"Nothing," I replied.

But Abigail cut in with, "Sophie's mum collects things

that other people have lost." I gave her a look to shut her up, but it was too late. She babbled on. "Like lost gloves and photographs left in library books and bits of paper people drop. Notes and stuff. She has lots of pennies, a massive jarful, right? And some really nice jewelry."

Megan twisted her lipstick back into the tube. "Weird," she said.

Abi seemed to realize I might be embarrassed because she flushed and glanced over guiltily. She said, even though she knows I don't smoke, "Do you want a cigarette?" as if it would undo her saying all that in front of Megan.

"No, thanks." I turned on my heel to show her I was still annoyed and slipped to the bathroom. I took a couple of deep breaths. I changed my shirt. The white one made my eyes look greener. I put on some more mascara— only on the top lashes like I read somewhere, so it doesn't smudge underneath. The doorbell rang, and people started arriving.

The back room was set up with the sofas pushed to one side so the DJ decks could be on the table by the patio doors. Zara showed up in a bright pink outfit that could look good only on her; the color would make me ridiculously pale. Megan's brother and some other guys dealt with the music. Soon cigarette smoke hung in the corners of the room like spiderwebs.

Abi and Megan twittered on. Both of them were drinking from the same bottle of vodka, completely wrapped up in their conversation. I wandered around. The two big sofas in the front room had loads of strangers squeezed between the cushions. I decided I'd rather sit in there than with Abigail and Megan, so I went in. A couple of guys shuffled over to make space for me. The nearest one asked my name and which school I went to, but I didn't want to talk so I gave him one-word answers. He gave up and talked instead to his friend. And here we get to the good part. Because I met a guy last night. (Me! I still can't believe it!)

So, I was sitting there, and he came into the room. He was at least six feet tall. He wore a shirt that said POP IT, and I read those words over and over, trying to work out if they were cool or dirty or what.

He CAME OVER and said, "I'm Dan."

I nodded. I couldn't speak. I was looking at his face. He had dark skin and blue eyes. I couldn't help but think that Emily would have noticed how great his eyes were. The color was the blue of those globes people sometimes have in their offices. Mum has one and most of it is ocean, and Dan's eyes reminded me of the globe on her desk. Except that color is flat and Dan's eyes had depth. Like his eyes had just been for a dip in the ocean. Blue, blue, blue.

One of the guys next to me got up and Dan asked if he could sit down.

"Sure." I smiled.

"I noticed you're not talking to anyone," he said, his voice deep and friendly.

"Um, maybe I'm shy?"

He smiled again like my answer was funny or sweet or something. "Let me see if I can help with that," he said.

My tummy tingled. And then we talked and talked. Here's everything I can remember. He's seventeen. He goes to St. Philips. He wants to study philosophy. He likes fried chicken because last year he spent a month in America somewhere and he ate lots of fried chicken. He wants to go traveling for longer next time: to South America and to Bali. When he said Bali, I thought about what had happened there and I froze a little, but he carried on speaking, so he can't have noticed. Um, so, he's from Iran. Well, he's not, his dad is, and his mum's from near me in Islington. And I wanted to ask if his parents were separated or together, and what Iran was like and if he'd been, and if his dad was Muslim, even though it makes no difference if he is because why would it? And I was thinking all these things, and I must have gone quiet because Dan said, "You're really pretty when you're thinking."

I just about fell off the sofa. It was like everything in the room stopped moving. All I could feel was my heart beating like a stuck needle in the groove of one of Mum's old records.

Abigail staggered in and sat on the arm of the sofa and wobbled to get her balance. She leaned over and said, slurring, "Dan, I see you've met my best friend, Sophie."

I crossed my arms and half turned away from her. I

wanted her to leave and stop flicking her hair and smiling at Dan. But he didn't really look at her. Instead he said, "So that's your name." Our eyes connected, and this shiver went ALL THROUGH ME.

Abi said, "I need to borrow her for a moment; is that okay?" She grabbed my wrist and pulled me into the other room.

"What's wrong?" I said. And then, "You're so drunk," which makes it sound like I was being mean, but I was just surprised. Abi hates getting drunk because of her mum.

"I feel really sick, Soph." She held her hand to her lips and said through her fingers, "Does vodka have loads of calories in it?"

"I'm not sure."

"I'm going to be sick."

"What do you want me to do?" I said.

"I don't want anyone to know."

I looked around at the older guys and everyone smoking and dancing. I thought how Abigail would feel being sick with all those people in her house. I took her to the bathroom and held her damp curls back while she threw up. The acid smell in the tiny space was nauseating, but when she was done, I stayed, helping her wipe her face and getting her some mouthwash.

By the time we got back downstairs, the party was loud with chatter and music. I looked for Dan, but I couldn't see him anywhere. I was tired and sad, and when I get like that

I don't want to be around anyone. I called a cab and it took ages for it to arrive. The driver overcharged me because he said *I'd* kept *him* waiting, which wasn't true, but I didn't have the strength to argue.

SUNDAY, JANUARY 15TH

Mum and I circled each other like cats today. It's almost as if she doesn't realize I've been back at school forever already. She kept asking if I have everything I need for Monday. I don't have anything I need, but I can't talk to her about that.

She just came in and sat on the end of my bed. Her eyes were empty of light: flat and sad. I didn't say anything. She didn't say anything, either, and just as suddenly as she'd come in, she left.

I got out of bed and followed her. She went into her office, shutting the door with a click. I listened to her crying for a while. I didn't want to go in there with all the lost things in her collection. My hands started shaking. I returned to my room and put the TV on loud enough to stop the thoughts in my mind going around and around like frenzied dancers.

I wish that I could fall asleep and make my brain rest. I've been lying awake for the last two hours. Mum's STILL in her room with her collection, and I don't want to go in there. It gives me the creepiest feeling even going past the door. Why is that collection so important to her? And what does it mean that she collects things that other people have lost? It's strange how in a home there are these questions that never get asked, things that never get said. I want to tell Mum to stop spending all her time in that room. I want her to come out and talk to me, but I don't know where we'd start.

MONDAY, JANUARY 16TH

I came home after school, and Mum was in the living room wrestling with the Christmas tree, trying to take it down. The tree was covered with brown needles that fell all over the floor as soon as Mum touched it. The little dead needles looked completely flammable, and I could just imagine the whole tree and Mum going up in a violent puff of smoke and flames. She would scream and collapse to the floor, struggling to breathe. I closed my eyes for a moment to clear away the image. I leaned against the doorframe with my hands in my pockets and thought about helping her, but then I remembered how awful Christmas day was. Mum didn't bother having turkey or anything— she doesn't cook anymore—and neither of us had bought presents. Mum said she couldn't imagine anything worse, so no presents. The stupid tree was only there because the

Haywoods had brought it over.

On Christmas day Mum and I sat in the living room and tried to think of things to say, neither of us able to say anything. I swear I could see Emily sitting on the other sofa making jokes and pulling faces, Mum laughing at her jokes. I screwed up my eyes and told my brain to stop.

Because it never would have been like that. Even before, Mum didn't laugh very often. She was always busy cleaning and tidying. If she ever sat down, her lips were squashed up tight as if she were trying to contain herself.

Once, years ago, a couple came for dinner. Mum's friends. Mum sat with her shoes off, kicked loose on the floor, her feet curled under her on the couch. She was drinking red wine, and her mouth got all purple. She gestured all about her, hands like birds, and she was laughing. She suddenly seemed like Emily: free and fun and happy. I bet when Mum was young, she was just like Emily. I think that's why she always loved Emily more than me, because she was like Emily when she was young. But she's not like that now. Not after years of looking after the two of us on her own, working full-time. Although she hasn't gone back to work, even though I've been going to school since the end of the summer.

I watched her yanking at the Christmas tree. Unable to bear it, I slipped out of the room and headed upstairs, where I put on really loud music.

Even over the music, I heard her yelling, "Sophie,

27

can't you see I need some help down here?" I know it was a terrible thing to do, but I turned up the volume and ignored her.

TUESDAY, JANUARY 17TH

School was long and boring. When I got home, Mum didn't even come out for supper. The only time I saw her tonight, her face was totally haggard. Worn away by time.

THURSDAY, JANUARY 19TH

We had this dance teacher come in specially today. He was the most crazy, intense guy on the planet. At only five foot three he was no taller than me. He wore cerise Lycra, and he was completely bald, which DID NOT go with the shiny outfit! He taught us this insane choreography. It started with two cartwheels, then a tombé and *sootanue* (or something), then a handstand from being on our knees, and finally hand gestures that he said were from sign language. It was all to this strange electronic music with beeps and whistles.

The only person who could do it was the new girl, Rosa-Leigh. The rest of us were trying hard even to remember what came next, and Rosa-Leigh could do it practically perfectly. He complimented her constantly. I was going to tell her how great she was when we sat for registration after lunch, but she was writing, maybe a poem, so I didn't.

I wonder what it'd be like to write a poem. I wouldn't even know where to begin.

TUESDAY, JANUARY 24TH

Emily went to my school before me. She was a star pupil, best of all at Art. I wish I'd never even chosen to do Art because the teacher, Mrs. Haynes, hates me. She sees Emily when she looks at me, I'm sure.

We had Art today. Mrs. Haynes wanted me to hand in my prep work. How stupid is that? To do prep work for a painting? Surely I should just do the painting, not sketch it first and waste time? I tried to explain to her that I didn't understand what a *sketch* was for and she yelled, "Sophie, we can't keep forgiving you for your failure to do the work you're given!"

I think she realized she'd gone too far, because her cheeks reddened. I've always thought she looked like a little witch with her sharp cheekbones and spiky hair, but in that moment she looked like a kid, all sorry and guilty. Then she looked like a witch again as she spat, "If you don't know what a sketch is, I can't see you ever passing your exam." She walked away, her spine stiff.

Abigail and Megan were sitting at the same table as me. Abigail must have been able to tell I was about to cry

29

because when I caught her eye she smiled over helplessly, as there was nothing she could do.

Rage fired through my body and heat roared like flames to my cheeks. I shoved my stuff into my bag, knocking my pencils onto the floor. Leaving them there, I started walking.

Mrs. Haynes screamed, "Where are you going?"

I kept walking, my cheeks hot as sunburn, and I let the door slam as I stormed out of the room.

Walking around school when everyone else is in lessons feels like walking around a cemetery. So quiet. My feet echoed down the white steps. I wondered what it might be like to climb white steps to heaven, if there even is a heaven. But I was going down. Getting farther from heaven with every step. Hot tears spilled down my cheeks. I pushed the double doors to go outside. It had started to drizzle.

The feeble rain dampened my shirt because I hadn't remembered my things. I hoped Abi would bring my jumper and blazer from the back of my chair where I'd left them. I rolled down my skirt so it covered most of my thighs. Shivering, I hurried toward the corrugated iron lean-to at the back of the field where Abi and I used to hang out, where she used to smoke and I used to chat. Abi and I spent so many hours back there planning for the future, talking about our families—her mum who drinks too much, my mum who worked too hard, talking about our sisters and her brother—talking about boys and school and everything. I need to make more of an effort with Abi. I'm the one who keeps screwing it all up. I'm surprised she still even likes me.

The field was squelchy with mud. I worried a teacher would be able to see me from the Addley Building. I imagined the music teacher over there running from her room and making me go back inside. No one came out. No one cared.

When I got to the lean-to, I expected it to be empty, but Rosa-Leigh was there, her arms wrapped around herself as she stamped from foot to foot. She was gazing out at the trees and didn't seem to have noticed me. I said, "What are you doing here?"

She shrugged. "I dunno. I could ask you the same."

"I hate Mrs. Haynes," I said, as if that explained anything.

She said, "I hate all of England. I wish I could go back."

"Me, too," I said.

"Go back where?"

"It doesn't matter," I replied, realizing how stupid I must sound.

She stepped to the edge of the lean-to and craned her neck to look at the sky. "It rains all the time here."

"I know."

"How do you live with it?"

"I guess I'm used to it," I said. Then, "I walked out of

Art. I'm going to get detention."

She said, "Don't you think it's dumb that we have to wear uniforms?"

"You don't in Canada?"

She shook her head, her hair sleek, even with the damp. I said, "I should go back."

"You can't if you walked out."

"I'm going to be in so much trouble."

"Don't worry about it." She picked up her bag. "You know, I didn't mean to be quite so . . . you know . . . unfriendly . . . when I first met you," she said.

"That's okay." I thought what else I could say. I ended up with, "It's hard starting a new school."

She smiled at me like she was grateful or something. I think she's really pretty; I wish I looked more like her. She said over her shoulder as she walked off, "I think if I stay away much longer Miss Sparrow's not going to believe I've been in the washroom."

I called after her, "You were really good at dance with that teacher," and then I worried that I sounded pathetic, but she was gone.

THURSDAY, JANUARY 26TH

Our house has a window from the upstairs bathroom that leads out to a flat roof. By scrambling through and sitting outside I can watch the comings and goings of the neighbors far below. I can see the tops of the nearby houses and the orange, starless skies of a North London night lit by trillions of street lamps. Passing cars send beams that lick the broccoli-shaped trees; a train thunders by, leaving darkness in its wake. I'm sitting here now, writing, even though it's cold enough to make my fingers feel brittle like bones with no skin or blood.

It was summer a year and a half ago. (I guess, although it feels like a different lifetime.) Emily and I clambered onto the roof long after Mum had gone to sleep. There were still hours to go before daylight, but that's what we'd planned to do: stay awake until the sun came up. Fluffy—I named her, evidence that originality wasn't my strong point (according to Emily)—came onto the roof with us and prowled along the edges, a shadow in the moonlight. We'd brought hot chocolate in a thermos and two sleeping bags, a small stereo. We put on an old Suzanne Vega CD, one of Mum's, something Emily liked to listen to. Vega does a song about sitting in a café, pouring milk, looking out of windows. Emily put it on Repeat.

Emily talked about interior designing, about art. She was going to Leeds College of Art & Design at the end of the summer. We talked about Mum. I reached out to forward the CD to a different track. One started about Christopher Columbus. I said, "He was Spanish, you know."

"Who?"

"Columbus."

"No, he wasn't," Emily said. "He was Italian." She looked at me as if daring me to argue. Three years, two months older, she always knew everything.

I didn't know what to say. After a long moment she said in her random way, "Do you know that the first person to survive going over Niagara Falls in a wooden barrel was a woman? Her name was Annie. The very first thing she said afterward was 'No one ought ever do that again.'"

I giggled. I put my hand over my mouth and tried to quiet down. "Why would *anyone* do that?"

"Imagine closing the lid, bobbing along a stupidly fast river, and then hurtling into space. It's either funny or terrifying."

"Or insane."

She said, "I read that she went over with a cat, which is the most insane thing of all."

I giggled again and this time couldn't stop. We both got the giggles. I remember looking at her brown eyes in the silvery light, her long blond hair held back with two pencils, her heart-shaped face, and wishing we could hang out more often.

We listened to the end of the album and set it to the beginning again. We played cards. Fluffy rubbed her furry head against Em's hand. We sat in silence for a while. I told Emily about a boy I liked.

"Steve at the end of our road? *That* Steve?" she said.

"He's cute."

"He seems really young. How old is he?"

"Sixteen. A year older than me!" I said.

"He doesn't look it."

"Well, I like him."

"Ask him out, then."

I thought about it, told her I might, knowing I was too scared ever to do that or ever follow through. I tried to imagine being a person like Emily, who could just ask out a boy if she wanted.

Then, far away, the sky began to lift. I said, "It feels like someone huge is peeling away the night, like God." Then I felt stupid. But she said she felt like that, too, that somewhere gods were endlessly painting and repainting the sky, sculpting clouds and moving them around, forever trying to make a perfect aesthetic. I didn't know then what *aesthetic* meant, but I didn't want to ask her. It was the sort of word she and Mum used together when they talked about art, when I sat there not understanding. I didn't know if Emily believed in God or not, but finding out right then felt like too big of a question. Of course now I wish that I'd asked.

Instead of watching the sunrise I watched her. She tucked her knees to her chest. Passing a pale tendril of hair between her fingers and her lips, she had a faraway look in her eyes. I turned to look at the sky, and a sliver of violently orange sun had been spat out of the roofs of the houses to the east. After all that waiting I didn't even see the coming of the day.

Today in detention Mrs. Haynes sat at the desk at the front, head down, scribbling away, holding the pen with such force I thought she would rip holes in the pages. Her face was all angry sharp angles. I tried really hard to imagine her as a teenager, what she'd be like if she was at school with me. I thought she'd probably be like Zara, all perfect clothes and perfect hair and nice teeth and bitchy sideways glances at everyone. The most annoying thing about Zara is that everyone (except me) deep down wants to be her friend, even though she thinks we're all immature. Right now she has a boyfriend who is eight years older. Thinking of that made me wish the guy from the party, Dan, had called.

Detention went on and on, and then, instead of thinking about Mrs. Haynes and Zara, I was all of a sudden thinking about sitting on the roof that time with Emily, and before I knew it detention was over. I had to go out in the rain and wait for the bus. Even though the bus took ages to come and it was freezing cold, time seemed to have gone all weird. I felt like I was back on the roof with Emily waiting for the sun to come up and I felt fine.

3

The silver of winter

THURSDAY, FEBRUARY 2ND

In the cafeteria today I bought myself chicken nuggets and chips. I sat with Abigail and Megan. The room was full, and I imagined what would happen if a fire started. The fire alarm would scream and water from the system would spray over all the panic below: girls running in every direction, trampling one another to get out. The heat and the smoke would layer over the fear like gravy over a roast dinner, suffocating.

Zara came over and plunked herself down. "God, the

day just goes on forever," she sighed. Everything she says comes out like she's sighing. I imagined her short black hair on fire, flames like devils dancing around her face.

She said, "Thank God I've got Alec. Isn't he adorable?" She says things like "adorable" all the time. She started telling us all the details of making out with Alec at the party. Not like we didn't see enough when we were there! I wish I didn't want to know, but I couldn't help listening. The others were rapt, too: Abi and Megan were paying so much attention to Zara, neither of them ate anything. When I asked Abi if she wanted one of my nuggets, she gave Megan this look like she knew something I didn't.

Megan said, "Not all of us can eat like you do."

My lunch tasted bad after that.

MONDAY, FEBRUARY 6TH

I had to go and see Lynda today after school. She called because I missed my last appointment and walked out of the one before.

No one knows—except Mum, who made me go in the first place—that I go and see her. That's one thing I have to be grateful for.

I forced myself to apologize. Lynda sat with her finger resting on her lips, her dopey face horribly sympathetic, and then said, "Take a seat and we'll forget all about it."

I wanted to leave again right there and then, but I made myself sit down. I said nothing else for the whole hour. She can't make me speak. Or remember.

THURSDAY, FEBRUARY 9TH

Tonight Rosa-Leigh and I waited for the bus FOREVER. We didn't say much to each other because it was raining and getting dark. We both had our shoulders hunched up. Cars streaked past, spraying rain over the slick pavements, and I imagined them suddenly veering out of control. Again and again in my mind's eye I witnessed cars crashing: the terror of the drivers, the agony of those last seconds as the vehicles slid out of control.

The bus came. As we got on, Rosa-Leigh and I bumped gently into each other. She smiled, in a nice way, and followed me to the backseat; normally, she heads upstairs.

She said, "Did you get detention for walking out that time?"

I nodded. "Surprise, surprise. But Mrs. Haynes is so stupid and mean that I don't even care. I'm glad. And I've done the detention already." I paused. "How was Miss Sparrow?"

"I like her, even though she seems a bit . . . you know. . . . She didn't even notice how long I'd been gone from class."

"I think she's weird," I said. "But I like English. I wish she were still my teacher. I had her last year. This year I've got Ms. Bloxam for English."

"Our form teacher?"

I pulled a face as I nodded. "She doesn't even like books," I said.

Rosa-Leigh said, "Have you read this?" She pulled a novel out of her bag. It was a Canadian book about a guy who loses his arm. It sounded really good, really different. She told me she reads a lot. Then she went quiet.

I said, "What?"

She pulled her mouth into a tight smile like she'd eaten something surprisingly bitter. She said, "My mom didn't really die like I said, you know."

I noticed grease on the window. Maybe from someone's hair wax. I thought about the person who'd leaned there. I didn't say anything.

Rosa-Leigh said, her eyes downcast, "Well, it wasn't like I said."

"So you lied?"

"Not exactly."

"Okay." I wanted to know what she meant, but it wasn't the easiest thing to ask.

She said, "Well, she did die, but it wasn't the reason I moved here, which is how it sounded when I told you. She died when I was really young."

"So why did you move here?"

"My dad got a new job."

"Why didn't you just say so?"

"I don't know. It doesn't matter."

"I don't really know what to say."

"I just wanted you to know. Mom died when I was two. I have a stepmom who's more like my real mom and she's not dead."

I couldn't help it. I had to put my hand over my mouth, and I was trying really hard not to, but I couldn't stop myself from laughing. It doesn't seem funny when I write it down, but there was something about the way she'd put all the words together that set me off. I said, "I'm sorry. I'm not laughing because your mum is dead," which sounded awful. But THANK GOD Rosa-Leigh's tight smile broke and she burst into giggles. That made me laugh more, so I was doubled over, laughing so hard it hurt, and she was laughing, and I kept trying to say it wasn't funny and we shouldn't be laughing, but every time I tried to say it, we both laughed harder.

Then I missed my stop, and we thought that was even more hilarious. Rosa-Leigh's stop was the next one. She said I should come over, and I figured why not.

As we got off the bus, it was pouring rain, so she ran, gesturing at me to follow. Rivulets made feather patterns on the slippery tarmac, all black and wet. We arrived at a big Victorian, three-floor house, redbrick with a red door. Because we were soaked, we slowed to catch our breaths, not caring that it was raining so hard. In the drive were a Mercedes Estate and a Citroen 2CV. Rosa-Leigh told me

41

what the cars were—I don't know stuff like that. The only car I know is the old Honda Mum has.

The 2CV was purple and yellow and really weird: all bubbly shaped. Rosa-Leigh said it'll be hers when she turns seventeen, which is in the summer like me.

She said, "And I'll be learning to drive on the left."

I wondered what it would be like to move to the other side of the world. England in winter has got to be awful to arrive into. I asked her what winter is like in Canada. She said that in Canmore, where she's from, it's cold for months and months of the year. Really cold. And really snowy.

We were so wet by then that water was trickling inside my shirt and tickling down my spine. I felt for a moment light and free, and I tipped my face up to the weeping sky.

Rosa-Leigh said, "This country's so rainy all the time. Come on!"

We hustled through the front door. I thought there would be just her and her dad and her stepmum and everything would be silent and dark around the edges with sadness because Rosa-Leigh's mum was dead. NOT AT ALL! Her stepmum came running down the stairs. She's tall and curvy, and she was wearing a low-cut red top that made her cleavage show, something my mum would never wear. Her walnut brown hair was incredibly shiny. She looked like she'd jumped out of the pages of a clothing catalog. She waved at Rosa-Leigh, smiled at me, said, "Hi, you're drenched!" and kept running toward the back of the house.

There were two doors off the corridor leading into brightly colored rooms. One looked like a playroom, full of carelessly thrown toys and books. The other was an elegant space that had three golden couches artfully placed under two huge paintings of mountains. A train set had been built on the coffee table, and the toy train lay on its side, clearly having careened to the floor. A faint smell of smoke hung over us. Rosa-Leigh's stepmum burst into the hallway holding a little boy she petted and told off all in the same breath. She said to us, "Hi. Sorry. Chaos. Sorry about the smoke everywhere. I burned tonight's lasagne. Disaster. Does it still smell terrible?"

From upstairs there came a shriek.

Rosa-Leigh's stepmum yelled, "That's enough, you two. You'll wake up Baby Adam. Oh, for goodness' sake." She ran up the stairs, holding the little boy against her waist. "Could you please leave it five minutes?" she cried.

Two guys came in behind us.

I looked at Rosa-Leigh. She must have seen the question in my eyes. She said, "I have a lot of brothers," and sighed affectionately.

The two guys were both older than me. One was maybe just a bit older, maybe seventeen or eighteen, and one looked more Emily's age, nineteen. They were black haired, like Rosa-Leigh, but with dark eyes. The older one had this twinkle in his expression like he knew *stuff*. He was laughing about something. The younger one was more serious;

43

his lips were thinner and pressed together.

Rosa-Leigh said, "Jack and Joshua."

I wasn't sure which one was which. They both said hi, then they reached out to shake hands, which seemed really formal. The younger one's hands were cold. The older one—Joshua, I think—held my hand for a second too long or maybe I held his hand for a second too long. My stomach did a little skip of pleasure. Then I felt weird because I really like that guy I met at the party, Dan.

Rosa-Leigh's stepmum came back downstairs, panting, but with a huge smile. "I keep trying to say hello properly. You must think we're dreadfully uncivilized!"

Rosa-Leigh pointed at the little boy in her stepmum's arms. "Andrew. And upstairs we can hear Aaron, Anthony, and Aiden." She went to get a hold of Andrew. "Angela and Dad like letter As, don't they? They'll run out of A names if they keep having babies."

Andrew squirmed out of her arms. His hair stuck up, he had crazy freckles all over his face, and his cheeks were flushed and rosy with sweat. He charged out of the hallway, hotly pursued by Rosa-Leigh's stepmum, who was laughing.

The guys went upstairs. Rosa-Leigh and I trailed into the kitchen. The warmth of the house was drying me off. I said, "How many brothers do you have?"

"Seven. Most are half brothers. Baby Adam's sleeping again, I guess."

Her stepmum reappeared. She shook my hand and said,

"I'm Angela. Sorry. It's a madhouse here."

She made us all a cup of tea. She asked about school and then told a story about little Andrew: he sat at the counter earlier in the day, ate a cookie, and said, "This is the life." She laughed as she told this; then there were shouts from upstairs. "How many times do I have to tell you boys?" she cried. Leaving her steaming mug on the counter, she disappeared out of the room.

"Your stepmum's so nice," I said. I suddenly remembered, "I should tell my mum where I am." I texted Mum. I didn't want to actually speak to her.

Rosa-Leigh was digging in a cupboard, and she called over, "I can show you photos of Canada if you like. I'll show you photos of my boyfriend."

"You have a boyfriend?"

"Not anymore. I told him we'd have to break up when I moved here." She took some photos out of a drawer and laid them on the counter. One was of her cuddled in the arms of this tall, cute guy dressed in winter sports clothes. She said, "He was a ski instructor."

She made us some pasta and sauce, so we ate that while watching a film called *Familia*, which is some random Canadian film about an aerobics instructor and her daughter moving in with another mother and daughter. Afterward, she showed me a poem she'd written about England and rain. I could picture everything in it, and I told her so. She let me read three more. One was about being in love with her boyfriend, and she told me it was out of date but she still liked it. The next was about them breaking up—it was harsh but brilliant, about a single lightbulb hanging from the ceiling of an empty room. In the last poem, which was what she called a prose poem, she wrote about the word *love*. She asked me about one of the lines. I made a suggestion, and she read the poem out again and liked the change. Prose poems are between prose and verse—maybe I'll try and write one.

It was getting late, and I still had homework to do, so I rang Mum because she hadn't replied to my text. She said she'd come and get me. I was surprised, but I wasn't going to say no and go back out in the rain and cold.

When Mum stood in the doorway at Rosa-Leigh's house she looked like a lost kid, small and wide-eyed. The expression on her face made me want to get out of there as soon as possible. Rosa-Leigh's stepmum asked us to stay and have a drink, but Mum must have felt the same way I did. Suddenly all the noise and people were too much. Mum said we had to go.

It was raining and dark when we got out of the car. Our street smelled of wet leaves. Mum said, "The worst time of the year," and her voice was tight, like it wasn't the worst time at all, like there were times that were far worse.

As soon as we got inside, I hurried up to my room. I flicked through the channels on the TV, but there was nothing on. In the end I switched it off. Then this sentence popped into my head about sticks and trees. I had to write it down. As soon as it was on the page, I wanted to write another. Ended up, I wrote a poem.

The sticks on the trees
Stand up harsh and bare
With rings on their fingers
And knots in their hair

The silver of winter
Is smoky with rain
The witches of sunlight
Fly low again

I think it'd be better if there was another verse but I can't think of one.

SATURDAY, FEBRUARY 11TH

Oh my God! Oh my God! Dan, the guy from the party with the blue, blue eyes, just called. He got my number off Megan and he called. Oh my God! He said hi, and then he asked if I wanted to do something on Friday, and I asked him what, and he said come to his house and hang out with him and maybe a couple of his friends. I said, "Yes!" (I tried to sound relaxed and not ridiculously excited.) Then we talked about school and films—I told him about *Familia*—until Mum made me get off my phone.

I pulled a face at her and said a quick good-bye.

TUESDAY, FEBRUARY 14TH

It's Valentine's Day, and I don't even have a boyfriend— well, not yet, but maybe soon. . . . I kept thinking about Dan and wondering if he might email or call, even though I spoke to him only yesterday and he's not my boyfriend or anything. Silly.

Poor Zara had a horrible day. Alec dumped her THIS MORNING. She was sobbing when I got into school. Apparently he's been seeing this other girl for SIX MONTHS. Abigail tried to cheer Zara up all day; she was really sweet. Even though she's loud and bossy sometimes, she has another side where she's thoughtful and kind. I haven't seen much of that side of her recently.

This evening I clambered onto the roof and thought about Valentine's Day two years ago. Emily was getting ready to go on a date with Ian. She was with Ian for the last two years of school. I was jealous of him because she never wanted to be with me anymore. Then, when she went to art college, she broke up with him anyway.

She was putting on this blue dress that emphasized her blond hair and dark eyes. I went to my room and searched through my drawer until I found my silver and sapphire necklace. I came back to her room and dangled it out.

"What?" she said.

"Wear this. It'll look good."

"What do you know about looking good?" she said, taking the necklace.

"Granny gave it to me," I replied.

She held up the necklace, then put it around her neck and pouted at the mirror. She smiled slightly, and I thought she was imagining Ian's face when he saw her later.

Oh God, I wish I could be back in that room with her. I'd give up everything—not that I have anything to give up. I'd cling to her so tightly, she wouldn't be able to breathe.

I looked at her. I said, "It suits you."

"Why didn't Granny give it to me?"

"You weren't here," I said.

And she's not here now. She's not here. How is that even fair?

WEDNESDAY, FEBRUARY 15TH

Everything has gone wrong.

School was okay; Rosa-Leigh and I hung out. She showed me another poem and we talked about that. We got the bus home and when I got in, Mum had collected supper, even though it was only takeaway pizza. We even talked a bit about school and stuff, although I only told her what I thought she'd want to hear. Then she asked who I'd been speaking to the other night, who'd made my voice go all soppy, and for about half a second it felt like old times when she was interested in me, so I told her that his name was Dan and I was going to his house on Friday.

She said, "But you can't. We have a long-standing arrangement with the Haywoods to go for dinner."

"I didn't know."

"There's no way you can get out of it."

"Just this once?"

"No, Sophie."

"I'm not a kid anymore."

"Don't start."

"I'm not starting. I just don't want to go." I pushed my plate to one side and stood up.

"You have to go."

"What for?"

"Do you think we need to argue about this?"

"I'm not going."

"You don't have any choice."

I knew there was no point to it, because once she'd said it was the Haywoods' house we were going to, there was no way I'd change her mind. Katherine Haywood is Mum's best friend from school, and they've been family friends forever, and their daughter, Lucy, is supposed to be my friend because we've known each other since we were little kids. Normally I wouldn't mind seeing them but not this Friday.

I leaned on the table to stop my hands shaking. "Please don't make me go. Please, Mum," I begged.

She shut her eyes. "We can't go on like this."

"Don't make this into something it's not. I just don't want to go to the stupid Haywoods'."

Mum said, "I'll take your phone and cancel whatever plans are suddenly so much more important than your family."

"What family?" I yelled.

"Give me your phone. If you don't do it yourself, I'll call." She was yelling, too.

"You're INSANE." I took my phone, went into my room, and slammed the door. I don't see why I have to go. They're Mum's friends. Lucy Haywood and I don't even have much in common these days. It's always uncomfortable when we hang out because we used to be so close when we were little. I even named one of my teddy bears after her when I was five. It's not that Lucy doesn't like me (I don't think) or I don't like her; more like once we were in the same fairy tale. The story had both of us in it, and all the magical adventures that happened, happened to us both. Now, we're not even in the same book: her book's more like a beach novel—conventional, ordered, following a predictable plot (boyfriend, school, great family)—and my book is like, well, it's not like that, anyway—not a romance, not a fairy tale, not easy reading for a summer day.

And the worst of it all is that Emily never had to go to

the Haywoods' when she had other stuff to do. But she always got away with everything, stuff I couldn't get away with if I tried.

I pressed in Dan's number. He didn't answer. I had to leave a message on his voice mail. Then Abigail rang and said she was going to Dan's house with some people on Friday and was I going? I felt stupid because I hadn't realized it was a *thing*—I thought it would be mostly just me and Dan, even though he said his friends would be there. I had to tell her no. Then we had nothing to speak about, because all I could think of was her sitting on the side of the sofa at her party, drunkenly flicking her hair and smiling at Dan.

THURSDAY, FEBRUARY 16TH

In Religious Studies today we talked about Muslims and the Koran. Megan, who I happened to be sitting next to, started saying that we should be careful how many of "Them" we allow into the country, and the way she said it was really nasty. And Kalila, who is a Muslim, got upset and said we were all racists. Zara sighed loudly and said we should all think about what we were saying. I wished I wasn't even in the room. If I could have made myself as small as an almond, I would have shrunk right down and sealed myself in a hard shell.

Megan said, "I'm not racist. I'm just looking at the facts. I'm talking about terrorists. We've got to keep ourselves safe—it's dangerous for all of us if we don't." She nudged my arm, "Sophie, you agree with me?"

My heart began to beat faster and my mouth went dry. All the colors in the room got brighter. I was thinking about terrorists and bombings and wars, and I wondered how someone could become a terrorist. An ordinary guy, going about his ordinary life, who is persuaded he'll get to sleep with however many white-clad virgins and live forever in some fluffy cloud if he just does this one thing. One murderous act. It makes as much sense to me as firing bullets into a crowd of strangers.

Kalila was looking at me, waiting for me to answer.

I stammered, "I don't know. Why would I know?"

Anger sliced through me. Not at bad things in the world like terrorists but at stupid, vicious Megan. I thought I might throw up. I had to run out of the lesson to the bathroom down the corridor. I was sick until there was nothing left inside.

I don't know what's wrong with me.

4

Is smoky with rain

FRIDAY, FEBRUARY 17TH

Dan STILL hasn't called me back. I wish he would. I thought he might. I keep checking my phone.

We're staying the night at the Haywoods'. I so don't want to go. I tried to say to Mum that I felt sick and shaky, but she told me to "Stop trying to evade your responsibilities." I want to go back to bed and sleep, because I've never felt so exhausted.

The times when Emily came with us to the Haywoods', we filled one whole side of their huge mahogany table that sits in their GORGEOUS room with big windows that look over their cool garden. When Emily was allowed not to go, Mum and I took up only two seats, and the Haywoods spread themselves out to fill the gap like they did this weekend. Trying to fill the gap.

Their house always smells of fresh baked bread and whatever else Katherine has been cooking—she's an amazing cook. Mum is much prettier than Katherine Haywood and thinner, and I wonder if when they were at school Mum thought her life would be better than her friend's. Maybe Mum never thought mean things like that. Katherine has yellow horsey teeth and a nonexistent chin. She tells jokes that aren't funny, but everyone laughs anyway. She's like a glowing hearth: she makes anyone who's near her feel warm. She works as a radio producer. Her husband, Mark, is brilliant and even I think he's good looking (although he's at least fifty). He always ensures Katherine has what she needs, even if it's only the salt. And then, as well as Lucy, there are the twin girls, Molly and Meredith, who are eleven now and SO ANNOYING but who make Katherine smile even more.

Lucy has bobbed hair, dyed purple right now, and lovely mahogany eyes that she puts perfect makeup around. I want to ask her how she learned to use makeup so well because one day she just seemed to have nailed it. She gets great marks at school and now has this really cute boyfriend called Kai. He was there for dinner last night, so it wouldn't have even mattered if I hadn't come. Lucy sat next to him all evening, their hands laced together. She seems to know what to say to guys (all of a sudden), and she's totally herself with him—I kept looking over and remembering how it was with *me* that she used to share all those little looks and giggles.

Mum must wonder why her family went so wrong. She must feel splattered with bad luck. As if there were a person sitting near us on the train journey of our life and this person ate too much from the buffet car. The buffet car on this particular train served up luck, both good and bad (on polystyrene plates). This person sitting next to us ate nothing but bad luck. And then, because he was totally full and because the train jolted going over a particular bump, he vomited bad luck all over us.

So, we were at dinner, sitting there, splattered with bad luck, and Katherine asked Mum how she was doing. Mum did this funny bright smile, glanced over at me, and said we were fine, much better.

Katherine looked at Mark and leaned over the table to put her hands over Mum's. She said, "You can always both come and stay here for a while, anytime—"

"No," Mum said. "Thank you, though."

I thought about staying in their beautiful house, looking

56

out over their beautiful garden, hearing the noise of all that family. I said, "I'd rather stay at home." I didn't say it loudly or anything.

Mum flashed a smile my way, but it didn't hide how tired she looked, like she hadn't slept in months. I wanted to reach out to her like Katherine had, but there was no way I was going to with everyone else there. Then I remembered that if it wasn't for Mum, I'd be at Dan's house, so I turned away.

Mark said to Lucy, "Why don't you take Sophie and Kai and show them the pool table?" Lucy jumped up. Then Mark said, "Molly, Meredith," and he didn't say anything else, and the twins skittered out of their seats.

A nerve flexed along Mum's jaw.

I said, "I've seen the pool table."

Katherine nodded. She waved a hand in my direction, but she was looking at Mum. "It's really wonderful. Lucy and Kai hang out there all the time."

Lucy tugged on my jumper sleeve, and I had no choice but to get up, too. My cheeks tingled as I reddened with irritation because I didn't want to leave. I'm sick of being treated like a kid, and they were so obviously trying to get rid of us. I followed her and Kai out. Just before the dining room door clicked shut, I heard Katherine say *my name*. I lied and told Lucy I was going to the bathroom.

She, wrapped up with Kai, went to the cellar. The twins had gone, so I was alone. I pressed my ear to the dining room door. What were they saying about me?

I couldn't hear very well.

Katherine: "You should. Sophie's obviously bottling everything up. She's doing a good job of pretending, but she's clearly not herself. And you need someone to help you." She said the next bit very gently. "You're both clearly struggling."

Mark: "We've talked about this. Let us help, please."

Mum: "It's so hard. I know what you're trying to do. I'm just so tired. And so alone. And so angry."

Mark: "We're angry, too."

Katherine: "Sophie seems completely disconnected. Does she talk to you at all? I can't imagine it. Poor darling is trying so hard to— Well, I'm not sure what she's trying to do. It's as if she wants to pretend nothing's happened. Have you talked to her? I can't imagine what this has done to her, but keeping it all inside is going to make things much worse."

Mum: "I can't bear it. I can't help her. I can't even help myself."

Then I missed a bit because someone put on the coffeemaker, and it whirred and percolated some of the words. As the mechanical whirring sound filled my brain, I imagined the coffeemaker blowing up and shards of glass and grains of coffee spraying all over the room, covering Mum, Katherine, and Mark with residue. I heard imaginary screaming, and I put my hands over my ears. My stomach clenched. Then Lucy scared the life out of me by clutching my elbow and spitting, "Don't."

The tops of her cheeks were red. She looked like she did when she was a kid. Once we spent an afternoon listing all the things we wanted for our tenth birthday, and it wasn't just material stuff; it was things like *nice nails, an end to nuclear arms, a boyfriend.* I couldn't imagine being that close to her again. She'd become a stranger I knew everything about. Like Abigail. Like all of my friends.

She tightened her grip. "Don't listen."

"I have the right to. They're talking about me. Why do they think I'm not coping?" I raised my voice. "I'm fine."

She gave me a long cool gaze. "Do you really think you're fine? How could you be?"

"What do you know?"

She blushed and lowered her eyes. When she looked back up, she acted like nothing had just been said. "Sophie, come with me. Come and have some fun. Kai's too good at pool—you can help me."

What I wanted to ask Lucy was if she missed Emily. If she missed the hours we used to spend playing together as children in her garden. And suddenly I felt really grown-up. And really, really sad. Mutely I followed her downstairs.

MONDAY, FEBRUARY 20TH

School was deathly. On the journey home I got soaked. Mum was out. I made myself a cheese sandwich with the last of the bread. I finished all my homework. No one called. I was so sick of my thoughts going around and around, I ended up writing a prose poem. It's a stream-of-consciousness thing. I'll show it to Rosa-Leigh tomorrow and maybe she can help me with it.

> **Burn**—*the word burn comes from fire, from heat, from lickety hot, flame orange like Halloween, and charred smoke stains like black soil once the forest fire is over, the earthy black remains. I remain turned outside in, the darkest corner of the forest opened to hot, wet light. I remain without you: a glass half full to everyone else, half empty to me.*

WEDNESDAY, FEBRUARY 22ND

I was supposed to hand in a personal essay for English today. The topic could be anything I wanted. Except I didn't do it. Now I have detention for tomorrow. If I get another detention, Mum will be called in to school to discuss my behavior. I don't feel like going to school ever again. I wouldn't care if I got expelled, but if I did, I'd have to deal with Mum, and that would be awful.

At break I gave Abi a top I'd bought her for her birthday. She said, "Can you come over early for my birthday thing the weekend after this?"

"You're having another party?"

"What's wrong with that?"

"Nothing. It's just, I don't know, you're having a lot of parties, but no, it's good. Yes, I'll be there."

She smiled when I said that, like I'd given her a gift voucher for a spa rather than a top.

I smiled back at her. My clockwork cuckoo smile.

"Is something wrong?" she said.

"Nothing. No." I wanted to ask her how it had been at Dan's when I was stuck at the Haywoods'. I wanted to moan about being given detention. But it was like the words got stuck along with all the other things I haven't said to her. To anyone. I thought of what Katherine had said about me being disconnected. But Katherine doesn't understand that it's better this way. I smiled brightly, too brightly, judging from the surprise in Abi's eyes. I said, "Everything's fine. I just haven't done that personal essay thing."

Megan came over. She must have overheard because she started talking about her stupid essay. She wrote about her dog dying. I couldn't believe it. Then she and Abi started talking about Dan's house. Even though I thought I wanted to hear about it, when Abigail said she spent all evening talking to Dan, my stomach churned. I wished she'd shut up.

Kalila was sitting by herself at the next table. Even though her head scarf shadows her face, I swear I saw her glance over, and she looked sorry for me.

Last night I went to Emily's room, opened the door, and stood there for a while before I went in. She has square mirrors all over one wall. I could see myself reflected in all those squares, and it was like lots of TV screens staring at me. I felt like I was waiting for something, like Emily might come out of the little bathroom in there, her hair flipped up in a towel, and yell at me to get out.

I went to her CDs all lined up on the blue wooden shelf and started looking through them. I hadn't even had two minutes looking at them when Mum came in. She said, "What are you doing in here?"

I shrugged.

She whipped around and started screaming, "Leave things alone. Don't touch anything. *DON'T!*"

I just stood there; I was so shocked.

She grabbed hold of my arms and pulled at me. I yelled at her to get off and tried to tell her I only wanted to borrow a CD. We got to the doorway, and I held on to it. She tugged at me, but I clung on. She went limp. Then she let me go and stared at me like I was a stranger.

I sobbed, "I wanted to borrow a CD."

She said, "Don't take anything out of there."

"Why?"

"I mean it," she said.

"You wish it was me," I replied, but really quietly.

Her face folded in on itself like I'd winded her and she couldn't catch her breath. Before she could say anything, I ran back to my room, slammed the door, and lay on the bed, frozen.

Mum knocked gently, and then, when I didn't answer, said through the door, "You know that's not true, right?"

I couldn't speak.

She said, "I'm sorry. I'm sorry about just now. I wish I could make this easier for you." I thought she said, "For both of us," straight after, but she must have started crying, because it was hard to make out her words. "Look, I know I need to do better for you. I promise I'll do better, Soph."

I wanted to say something; I really did.

She knocked again and said, her voice choked, "Can I come in, Sophie?"

I thought she might push open the door but she didn't. She didn't come in. I hate her. And I hate Emily for making all this happen. I can't believe I just wrote that. But it's true.

TUESDAY, FEBRUARY 28TH

Rosa-Leigh and I decided to walk home today because it wasn't quite as cold as it has been. She asked me to come to her house on Friday, but I'm going to Abigail's thing, so I had to say no. It was a looooooong walk. We came up through the park and went through the maze and got lost, which was kind of fun. Afterward we sat on the grass and watched the grey skies darken. She started talking about how the air glitters with specks of frost in Canmore in winter. She spoke about sun dogs. I made her describe them to me: some weird weather thing where the sky looks like it has three suns. Then she started talking about her mum. She doesn't remember very much, just stuff from photos mainly. She asked me, "Could you listen to a poem I wrote about her? Can I read it to you?"

I nodded. She read to me quietly. As I listened, I started thinking about my mum and the terrible fight on Sunday night. Mum is obviously insane. She clearly hates me and can't cope with Emily not around. She doesn't seem ever to want to go back to work. She used to love designing. She made people's homes beautiful with soft fabrics in shades of green and earthy orange. Her style was very organic, Emily told me once. Emily had a jazzier artistic eye. She would mix all sorts of colors and make everything come together; she loved the texture of oil paint. I never knew what to say when they talked "*Art*" together; I don't have an artistic eye at all.

Rosa-Leigh finished her poem. I made her read it to me again, and I concentrated harder. The cold seeped like misery into my bones. The grass smelled damp, composty. With her poem Rosa-Leigh conjured a picture of her mum in the earthy air. I shivered as she finished the poem for the second time. I said, "That was beautiful." I felt stupid for saying it straight out like that, but it was true and Rosa-Leigh didn't seem to mind. Then I took a deep breath and said, "My mum collects things that other people have lost."

She leaned back on her elbows and said, "Why?"

"I don't even know. She's always done it. Even when my sister was still around. I think even when my dad was alive, but I can't really remember. She has gloves and a couple of socks, which are disgusting, and she's really proud of her single earrings. It's so weird—no one in the WORLD collects stuff other people have lost."

"What happened to your dad and your sister?"

I couldn't believe she didn't know about Emily. My insides became a fist. "Dad died when I was little. He had cancer, but I was too small to really know him. I was only two. It was always just me and Mum. And Emily . . ." I had to pause before I started the next bit. I said, "My sister . . ." I didn't finish.

She was quiet. I heard a rustle as she lay back completely. She said, "Look up."

I copied her and lay down. The sky spun with my dizziness.

She said, "Can you see the stars coming out? You don't get so many stars in London."

I said, "I miss her all the time."

"Are you okay?"

I stared straight up, blinking back tears. "I think so. I'm fine."

"What else does your mum have in her collection?"

"Newspaper articles about stolen babies and about people who've gone missing. There's a gold medal, and I don't know what else. I haven't been in there for ages."

Rosa-Leigh said, "I wonder what my mom was like."

"How did she die?"

"She was hit by a drunk driver. I wish that I could remember her. Joshua and Jack talk about her sometimes. That's how I could write the poem."

"It was really good."

"Thanks. It makes me feel better when I write."

I didn't say anything. It started to drizzle. When we sat up, the rain looked liked slivers of glass in Rosa-Leigh's hair. Eventually we were so cold, we decided to pull each other from the ground and finish the walk home.

WEDNESDAY, MARCH 1ST

Mum went out tonight to some support group thing that she suddenly announced she was joining, smiling at me like I'd be pleased. I still haven't forgiven her for yelling at me the other day, so I didn't say anything, but I was surprised.

After talking about her collection with Rosa-Leigh, I wanted to go and sneak a look once Mum had gone. I opened the door to her office. She used to have all her interior design work on her desk, but now her collection has taken over most of the room. I couldn't even see the desk for the jumble of things. I swear she didn't have that much stuff before. The room is TOTALLY full. It's chaos in there. Scattered everywhere are raggedy bits of clothing. A teddy bear with one eye lies on the floor, and a jar full of pennies sits on her chair. Mum is obviously losing the plot.

I can't stop thinking about what the Haywoods said. They said we should go and stay with them. I don't know if that would help Mum. Should I be worried about her? Maybe the Haywoods should know that her collection is getting out of control. I closed the door behind me and hurried down to the living room.

I fell asleep on the sofa while watching TV. I dreamed I was in a small dark space with a fire coming closer and closer. I couldn't get out. I woke sweating.

Mum still wasn't home. I clambered up the stairs to my room. My head felt like it might explode. I have to stop myself thinking about anything. If only I knew how. At least our half-term holidays start tomorrow. I couldn't face going to school.

5

The witches of sunlight

FRIDAY, MARCH 3ʳᴰ

Abigail called and told me Dan called HER last night. She
was so excited—just gushing. I'm too depressed to write. And
JEALOUS. Why would he call her and not me? Although
he told her he wasn't coming to her party so maybe that's a
good thing, right?

I'm just about to go to Abi's house for her birthday thing.
I'm staying the night. I'm going to have to listen to her
going on and on about him all evening.

Abi gave me a huge hug when I arrived and pulled me upstairs to her room. She whispered that her mum had been drinking. "Even though she promised she'd go out, she's in bed sleeping."

"Are you okay?"

She pulled a face and said, "I'm fine. What are you going to wear tonight? Do you want to borrow my black jeans?"

I fingered through her clothes and listened to her chatter. I tried on her jeans and decided I didn't like how they looked, so I took them off and put my own jeans back on. She smoked and the air in her room grew thicker. She kept saying how skinny I was and how great I looked. In the end I just gave her a look to tell her to stop.

She said, "What?" but she stopped. She put on loads more makeup than she usually does. Zara came in. I was surprised because it was still early and Zara is always late. She wore a black hat and a fantastic purple dress that would make anyone else look overdressed. I wish I could wear hats and look cool but I can't.

So, Zara came in and said, "I had to come early because I had to get out of my house. My mum is crazy."

I wanted to say that if she thought her mum was crazy, she should try mine, but I didn't say anything.

She took a cigarette from Abi's pack, lit it (apparently she smokes now), and continued, "My mum caught me and Alec"—they're back together; she's forgiven him—"in bed together." She blew a smoke ring. "She's furious."

I was glad I hadn't said anything, because Zara obviously meant crazy angry, not crazy *crazy* like an insane person. Then she went on for ages about stuff she'd done with Alec. I both wanted her to shut up and to tell us more. Everyone has done it EXCEPT ME—even Abigail, but she used to say she regretted it. Now she acts like she knows EVERYTHING. She shared all these knowing looks with Zara.

Zara said, "Where's Megan?"

I shrugged.

Abi said, "She'll be here." She smiled at Zara. Because I felt so excluded, I ignored them. Then Abi got it into her head that we had to make cupcakes for the party. Zara and I were like, "We're not five years old," but Abigail insisted. Then Zara decided it was a good idea (which surprised me because usually she's so cool and aloof), so we went downstairs and whipped up this mix and made cakes and put them in the oven. It was kind of fun, but by the time we had to ice them, we'd had a couple of drinks. I ended up icing all the cupcakes by myself, because Zara and Abigail went outside to smoke pot. I felt kind of tipsy and didn't want to get stoned, too. I poured myself another vodka. Then Megan came in from the back. I didn't know she'd arrived. She said, "You've been making cupcakes."

I nodded.

She said, "God, I wish I could have one."

I said, "Have one. I don't know if the icing has set yet, though."

Megan shook her head and put her hand on her stomach. "I don't think so."

I finished covering the cakes with this neon yellow icing, and I scattered sparkly sugary things over them. People started showing up, but no one ate any of the cakes, so it had all been a waste of time. I got into a conversation with Zara, which never happens, and she talked about boys—surprise, surprise—and was midway through telling me a story about Alec when her phone interrupted.

I went outside. There were some guys there, and I stood around watching them smoke a joint but refused it when they passed it to me because I was still feeling a bit drunk. I wished for a moment that Dan were there. I remembered his blue eyes and his smile. I went back inside because it was freezing outside and saw there were some more boys smoking pot inside.

I went to let Abigail know. Her mum is pretty laid-back—or just doesn't care—but she won't let anyone smoke pot *inside* her house. Just as I found Abigail, her mum appeared at the top of the stairs all bleary-eyed and wobbly. She used to be a ballerina, and she's very elegant and thin. She normally wears her black hair in a bun, but because she'd been sleeping, it was loose and frizzy, sticking up on one side. Her red lipstick was smeared. She started yelling, "Get everyone out! I can smell marijuana. Abigail, get them *out*." It would have been funny if it was on TV, but it was really happening. Everyone stared.

Abigail yelled at her mum, "How could you do this to me on my birthday?" and she was crying.

"This isn't a drug den, it's my home!" Abi's mum screamed. The muscles in her skinny throat tensed and her collarbone was sharp and angry.

Then they were both yelling. People emptied out of the house like rats leaving a sinking ship. There was no one left, not Zara, not even Megan. I stood there unsure what to do with myself. Abi turned to me and said, "Please go. I don't want you here. This is so embarrassing."

I felt tears springing to my eyes, and I turned away before she could see. I got my coat, but then she grabbed me and said, "I'm sorry. Please stay. I need your help." She gestured at her mum, who was now sitting slumped on the bottom step. We got her up to bed, which was like leading a staggering foal, all long limbs and falling over.

When we finally got to bed, I wanted to talk to Abi, but she went straight to sleep. I lay there for a long time, unable to drift off.

SUNDAY, MARCH 5TH

DAN EMAILED ME!!! I thought, since he hadn't called back, I wouldn't ever hear from him again. Maybe he sensed I was thinking about him!

It says:

Sorry I wasn't at the party this weekend. It would have been good to see you.

I like it because he hasn't cut any of the words short like people do in emails, as if they're not really words. (Why do I care about stuff like that? What's wrong with me?) His email makes me want to know so many things. Like, how did he get my email address? Did he just email me or did he email everyone else? No, definitely just me: he says it would have been good to see me! He wouldn't have written that to everyone. Abi would know, but I feel weird asking her right now. Yesterday morning she was distant. She didn't eat breakfast, although I made us both eggs on toast. She said she was too hungover and depressed. I wanted to tell her she had nothing to be depressed about: at least she still has her sister around.

I wish I hadn't just written that.

TUESDAY, MARCH 7ᵀᴴ

Lynda asked me what I'd written about Emily recently. I didn't answer. She told me I had to take the diary seriously to stop me blocking out what had happened. I felt heavy, and I couldn't look at her. I said, "I'm not blocking anything out." The sentence emerged like I was in a room filled with thick smoke, each word hurting my lungs.

Half-term over and back to school today. Yuck.

I went to sit on the roof after I'd done my homework tonight. Normally you can't see many stars from up there, but tonight the sky was full of them, like little needle marks in a swathe of black fabric. It made me remember something that happened with Emily years ago, and I was glad I'd brought my notebook up with me so I could write and write.

I remember the sky was punctuated with stars that night, too. We were out somewhere, we'd gone to watch fireworks, and Emily had just said she was hungry. Mum said to her that we should all get baked potatoes. Emily must have been thirteen. She seemed to have forgotten her hunger and was making eyes at a boy. Mum, oblivious to Emily primping her lips, pulled us toward the food stand.

A man was hunched over, busy opening hot potatoes wrapped in silver foil. Someone shouted through a loudspeaker that the Catherine wheel was about to start. The man asked if we wanted something, impatiently tapping his fingers. He clearly thought we'd want to watch, but all three of us thought Catherine wheels were *boring*, the way they stay fixed to a fence or tree and just spin around and around shooting out sprays of sparks. Most of the time they don't even work! Even Mum thought they were boring, although she always said, "Only boring people get bored."

We paid, and the man turned his attention to the throng-ing crowds, reaching up on his tiptoes to see the Catherine wheel (probably) sputter and die.

I took my potato, filled it with butter and cheese, and mashed the insides with a plastic fork. Emily got hers and did the same thing; so did Mum. Sometimes we were so alike. The air was cold, and the potato warmed my palms. I breathed the smoky smell of bonfires and rotting leaves.

The loudspeaker announced that the fireworks were about to start. The three of us rushed over toward the front row of the firework display, dodging between groups of teenagers and families bigger than ours. I put a forkful of hot potato to my mouth, but before I got any, someone knocked my elbow. My potato fell to the ground. I hadn't eaten a bite. I looked at it lying there, muddied. I chucked away my fork in frustration.

We didn't have time to get back to the man selling food before the fireworks started. We got to the front row. As the first firework exploded in the sky with a bang, tears welled in my eyes. I wanted that potato so badly. Emily looked at me; I felt her gaze. The last thing I needed was some smart comment from her. Without a word she gave me her potato.

I took it, feeling the warmth through my fingers. She passed me her fork. I didn't look at her. I ate the whole thing, never saying thank you.

I should tell Lynda I don't need help and stop going to our appointments. She said writing it down would help. I feel worse right now. Worse than ever.

FRIDAY, MARCH 10TH

This evening I saw Mum go into Emily's room and close the door. I felt as lonely as an empty plastic bag. It took me ages to get my breathing under control.

SATURDAY, MARCH 11TH

I went to Rosa-Leigh's house. When we arrived her stepmum gave us a cup of tea, and we chatted with her for a few minutes. Andrew was at a playdate, so she wasn't running around after him. She said, "I remember when I was your age and the whole world felt like it was opening up to me. It was—" Her phone rang, so she didn't finish the sentence.

If there had been time, I'd have told her the world wasn't opening up, rather closing like a flower when the sun goes down. I'd have said the world sometimes feels completely closed, like Emily's bedroom door.

Rosa-Leigh elbowed me in the ribs and said, "Cheer up."

"Sorry," I said.

"Come and help me finish unpacking."

"You haven't unpacked yet? It's been months!"

"Yeah, yeah."

We ran up to her room in the attic. It's like a tree house up there, perched at the edge of the last step. Rosa-Leigh has painted it cream. Since I was last there, when we watched *Familia* together, she's painted a mural on one of the walls. It's a street scene with people and animals walking along.

"You really painted this?"

She nodded.

"My sister would have loved it."

She was quiet. Then she said, "I'm glad. Now, help me with all these boxes."

MONDAY, MARCH 13TH

Rosa-Leigh gave me a magazine called *The New Yorker*, which is American (obviously). She wanted me to read the poems. There were two. I've never seen a magazine with poems like this. One of them is all about a train stopped at a station. The poem describes seeing into someone's open front door from the train window. It's also about cornflowers, which are blue. The whole poem makes me feel like I can see blue cornflowers inside a woman's front door. And like I'm waiting for something.

77

After I read it, I wanted to write a poem myself.

Seconds are slipping through my fingers
Small silver fish through a net
Heat in my cheeks, like winter
Sun in my face, summer gone
The fisherman can't catch everything
In an empty ocean;
In an empty ocean
Small silver fish swim.

I know it doesn't make sense, because in an empty ocean there can't be any fish, but I like how it sounds—all deep and cold. I don't really think it's finished. Maybe the last line would be better if it said, "Small silver fish *can't* swim."

When I write a poem, I feel good for the whole time it takes. The rest of the time, I don't know what I feel. I don't want to feel anything at all, really.

Mum just pushed open the door and asked if we could talk. I was surprised, but so awkward with her, I didn't know what to say. "What?"

She said, "Are you all right, Sophie?"

"Why?" I said. If I even feel normal for a minute, she wants to ruin it. Anxiety bubbled up in my stomach like acid, so I had to take a slow breath.

She said, "You can talk to me."

78

"I don't want to talk. Not to you. Not to anyone. I'm fine. I've got loads of homework, so . . ."

She sighed heavily, and after a long UNCOMFORT-ABLE pause she left. I lay on the bed for ages trying not to think about anything. I fell asleep in my school uniform. I peeled my clothes off in the middle of the night because I was in a cold sweat. Maybe I've got a virus.

THURSDAY, MARCH 16TH

School boring. Mum's giving me a lift over to Abigail's for dinner. I wouldn't have accepted the lift from her because things are so strained right now, but I didn't see any other way of getting there. At least Abi's older brother is home for a couple of weeks, back from traveling in Peru or Ecuador or somewhere. He's always got an interesting story, and even though Abi's sister is away at university, it'll be good to hang out at their family dinner. Hopefully her mum doesn't drink too much.

Dinner was a disaster. When I arrived, Abi's mum was knocking back vodkas, already totally hammered, struggling to focus but still managing to make really dirty jokes that weren't funny. I was amazed there was food on the table, but she seemed to have managed the cooking all right. I wondered for a moment how Abi felt with her mum in such a state. She must be embarrassed. Then Abi told me her brother wasn't EVEN THERE. After we'd eaten, Abi and I went upstairs to her room.

She stood in front of her shelves and pulled out the white shirt I like. She said, "You can have it."

"Thanks."

"It wouldn't fit me now anyway." She put her hands on her hips and sighed.

"What do you mean? You're thinner than you've been for years. It'll totally fit. It'll look good."

"God, Sophie, you're so—"

"So what? I'm so what?"

"Just, you know."

"I told you the shirt would look good on you."

"You don't understand what's going on. You never do."

I said, "Give me a break, Abigail," which I think is what Rosa-Leigh would have said.

"I'm always giving you a break nowadays."

"What do you mean?"

"You know what I mean."

"No, I don't."

"Just take the shirt and forget I said anything," she said.

I threw it on the floor. "I don't even want your stupid top."

"Get over yourself, Sophie."

"You have no idea what it's been like," I mumbled.

She hissed, "How am I supposed to have any idea what it's been like? You won't even talk about it. What do you want me to do? It's sad and horrible and awful, and I don't know what else to say. And you won't help me out."

"Help *you* out? What do you mean help *you* out? How can you be such a bitch? I've always been the one who helped you out. I've always supported you and been there for you, and you just can't do it for me."

"Is that what I am? A bitch? And what about you? When have you got time for anyone else? You don't even know what's going on." She started crying. Mascara ran under her eyes like smears of black ash.

"I can't believe you'd do this to me. I can't believe you'd be so selfish!" I cried. "You have no idea what it's like. ALL THE TIME."

"I can't handle it anymore."

"Can't handle what?"

"You!" she yelled.

"Why are you doing this to me?"

"I'm not doing anything," she said.

"You're screaming at me. TYPICAL. Abi, you're so wrapped up in yourself, you're so selfish. You've always been like this. You're always the one we have to worry about and talk about, and now that all this has happened to me, you can't handle it because you're so SELF-INVOLVED. Nothing bad has EVER happened to you. You don't have ANYTHING wrong in your life, and you can't handle that I might need a bit of support."

"Bad things are happening in my life, not that you'd

notice. And how am I supposed to support you when you won't let me? You won't even TALK about it!" she screamed.

"I don't WANT to talk about it. I don't even want to THINK about it." I was crying now, and I grabbed my bag and ran downstairs.

Abi's mum was hovering in the hallway. She said, completely slurring her words, "What's going on?" She wiped her black hair from her face and smiled sympathetically at me.

"I'm going home. I'm sorry." I was really crying.

She called upstairs, "What have you done, Abigail?"

"It's nothing, Mrs. Bykov," I said. "I just want to go home." I opened the front door and ran outside. It was dark and cold. I ran to the train station at the end of Abi's road. I got to the ticket kiosk, and I started shaking. My body trembled all the way through. The man behind the ticket window said, "Where are you going?" The fluorescent lights made everything a terrible grey, the grey of a morgue.

I heard a train rumble onto the platform. From where I was standing, I could see it pulling in. Nausea rose at the back of my throat. I looked back at the man. I couldn't breathe.

He said, "Are you all right?"

"I've changed my mind," I said. I pulled my phone out of my pocket, trying not to drop it, my hands were shaking that much. I said, "Have you got a number for a cab?"

"I'll call you one," he said.

I felt momentarily grateful, and then so shaky and sick I could hardly think. The whole cab ride was a blur. When I got home, I called out a quick hi to Mum and went straight to my room. My mouth was so dry that I thought drinking water would help, but I only felt sicker. I thought I was dying. I wanted to scream to Mum that I was having a heart attack, that something terrible was happening to me, but I was too frightened to call out. My heart was hammering like a woodpecker in my chest, in my neck, in my throat, and it was the loudest thing in the world. Even with my fingers in my ears, I couldn't block out the sound. I moaned a little and curled up on the bed.

Hours later—or was it minutes? I have no idea—my breathing slowed down, and the crazy thoughts stopped whirling through my mind. I don't know what had even happened to me. Am I going mad?

6

Fly low again

FRIDAY, MARCH 17TH

Dan CALLED this morning, but I missed his call, and I'm
too shy to call back—what would I even say? I got to school,
and Abigail wasn't speaking to me but I don't even CARE.
At least my heart is beating normally now.

SATURDAY, MARCH 18TH

I slept badly last night. I was having the worst dreams. I

dreamed I was giving birth to these horrible creatures all made of fire, and they screamed as they were born. I woke up, and I was having my period. I hate periods. They just seem the most stupid, pointless thing for someone who's sixteen. I don't want to get pregnant (not that there's any chance of that, even if I did want to). No sixteen-year-old in the universe wants to get pregnant, so WHY do we have periods? Some girls start when they're ten. Why does a ten-year-old need to have a period? Mine is so irregular I can never predict it, which is a nightmare.

I had bad cramps, and I lay there with a hot water bottle, watching TV. My weekends used to be so full and busy. I'd go to trampoline class first thing on a Saturday, then judo, then drama on Saturday evenings. After, I'd go to Abigail's or she'd come to mine. Then Sundays we'd wake up together and make breakfast, and we'd hang out or go shopping or something, and then we'd do homework until it was time to go home. But Abigail didn't call today and I'm not going to call her.

I watched an episode of a soap I've never seen before. I cried when someone called Ness broke up with this cute guy Martin because she had cancer and was dying. Then I switched channels and watched a DISGUSTING documentary about female bodybuilders.

After the bodybuilding thing the news was on, and there was another suicide bomber in Afghanistan. Twenty-five people murdered. Just like that. Because that's how it goes: people die and there's nothing that can be done. The edges of the world seemed suddenly darker. My heart slammed against my ribs. How can the world be like this? Why do people do such terrible things? It doesn't make any sense. I couldn't breathe. I threw up. Even that didn't make me feel any better.

We're going to the Haywoods' for the rest of the weekend. Katherine must have taken pity on us because, when she called just now, I answered the phone and I was really bored and down and Mum probably sounded no better. She invited us straightaway.

SUNDAY, MARCH 19TH

We're just back from the Haywoods'. I spent most of the time spinning like a third wheel with Lucy and Kai. Seeing them together made me think about Dan, which is completely stupid. I wish I had someone, though. I wish it were Dan. I haven't heard from him since I missed his call. I wonder if I should call him back.

This weekend I found out Lucy has a blog. It's strange that she tells the whole world everything that happens to her while she can't seem to find the words to tell me anything. I can't imagine writing a blog and putting all my secret thoughts out there for everyone to read. I did create my own blog once but I couldn't write a word. It was like

86

someone was holding my hands behind my back; the idea of all those people out there being able to read it just killed me. Loads of people do it. I know annoying Megan does, but hers is *so* ridiculous that it makes me want to pass out. She has stupid pretend names for everyone, and it's all this stuff about her boring life. She once wrote something about Abigail (using the name Annabel), and Abigail went mad.

It's weird not being friends with Abigail.

Lucy's blog is better than Megan's. She won an award for it, and loads of people read it. I'll try and remember to take a look.

Mum spent lots of time with Katherine. They went to a Pilates class, followed by lunch. Mum even smiled once. No one said anything about us moving in with them. I don't know if I was happy about that.

TUESDAY, MARCH 21ST

I climbed out on the roof tonight. It was chilly and lonely, but I settled myself down and started writing.

I remember Emily holding my hand one time, maybe two and a half years ago. We were on a family holiday in Greece, and Mum was off looking at some old ruin. Emily and I were sitting close together in a café on the beach. She talked about a cute boy walking past. She'd taken my hand without thinking, it seemed. She let go when the food arrived. We ate a Greek salad—Greek salads smell of Greece to me: all fruity tomatoes and sharp feta and the warm smell of fresh basil; she had the olives because I hate them—and saganaki, a fried cheese that we both adored.

Later we sat on the beach for the final moments of the day. We both loved sunsets. The sun melted into the sea. The light bounced off the water, making the surface of the ocean look like the scales of a fish. I wondered aloud what it would be like to be a mermaid. Emily laughed at me but not unkindly. I moved closer to her on the sand. I reached for her hand, but she brushed me off. The next day we left for home.

THURSDAY, MARCH 23ʳᵈ

ABIGAIL IS STILL NOT SPEAKING TO ME. I tried to make up with her today by writing her a letter to say I was sorry about the stupid fight. She spread it out on the table and read it OUT LOUD to Megan and Zara. Rosa-Leigh came in, saw what was happening, and steered me out of the lunchroom. I'm so ridiculous, I started crying. I kept apologizing to Rosa-Leigh for being so upset, but she said I shouldn't apologize for being sad.

The afternoon went by really slowly. I wish more than anything I hadn't taken Art. I hate it. I wish I could have done Creative Writing instead. On the bus I showed Rosa-Leigh the poem I wrote a while ago about silver fish. She smiled, in a good way. She showed me some poems she's been working on, and we talked about them. She sent me some music this evening: it's a Canadian band she likes a lot. The singer is a woman, and she has this weird, cool voice.

SATURDAY, MARCH 25TH

Just as I'd given up hope, Dan emailed and this is what it says:

Sophie, do you want to come to my house tonight? I'm having a party.

I've read it a million times. Now I have to work out what to wear. I really hope Abigail's NOT THERE. I called Rosa-Leigh to see if she wanted to come with me. Her dad's giving us a ride. I pressed the phone against my ear, suddenly wanting to cry, even though I had nothing to be sad about.

Rosa-Leigh wore a black short dress over jeans. Her hair was loose, and she looked amazing. I wore a silky blue top and jeans, and Rosa-Leigh said I looked awesome, too. She gave me these earrings made of jade to borrow, just little and green, but they went really well with my eyes.

Her dad dropped us off at Dan's. Through the curtains, we could see the silhouettes of people packed in the front room. I knocked on the door and someone yanked it open.

It was one of those houses where the front door leads right into the living room. All the excitement I'd felt on the way over just disappeared. I was like a balloon with all the air coming out, except I didn't make that noise. Because Abigail was at Dan's. Along with Megan and Zara.

Abi saw me with Rosa-Leigh and gave this laugh and then leaned in to talk to the other girls. They all huddled together so I couldn't hear what they were saying. Dan sauntered into the room. He came over and hugged me. My stomach danced and tingled. (Also, I was pleased because Abigail was watching and so were all the others.) He lightly kissed my cheek, and I could smell beer really strongly. He pulled back and tried to look at me. His eyes were red and fuzzy from drinking, but he was still really cute.

He said, "I'm glad you're here."

I nodded, my heart skipping, and introduced him to Rosa-Leigh. Rosa-Leigh said a quick hello then led me through into the kitchen. It smelled of sticky punch and of sweat. She leaned against a laminate counter filled with bottles, and pulled a *he's-the-guy?* face.

"What?"

"He's drunk. Really drunk."

"I like him." I realized as I said it that I *really* like him.

Abigail came into the kitchen and saw us. She went straight back out and then came in again with Dan, her arm through his. She flicked her frizzy hair, pouting up at him, and COMPLETELY IGNORED ME. While she started pouring drinks for the two of them, he stumbled over. "How've you been?" he asked.

"Um, okay," I said. I'm so pathetic.

He smiled and my silly heart flopped about like a fish out of water. He tried to say something, but he got lost in his words because he was a bit too drunk. And then, I SWEAR, Abigail squeezed between us even though he was trying to talk to me, pushed herself up against him and started kissing him RIGHT THERE.

Dan raised his eyebrows like he was shocked, but it didn't stop him kissing her back. A jealous ache went right through me; I wanted so badly for him to kiss me like that. I couldn't believe what was happening. I wanted to burst into tears, or pull her off, or say something, but I didn't do anything. Rosa-Leigh had her hand pressed against her mouth and I could tell she was going to die from horror if we didn't get out of there. She seemed to realize that kiss was like a knife in my back, so she pulled me into the living room.

I said, "I can't believe Abi just did that."

She said, "I can't believe Dan did. Let's get out of here."

We were going to leave, but Zara called me over and said she thought my top was adorable, trying to be nice, I guess. Then Abi came in smirking and pulled Zara off to one side. By then there were loads of people in the house.

Rosa-Leigh came over and whispered in my ear, "I've got a better idea. Really, let's go."

Out in the cool night the sky was crisp. We could see our warm breath, cloudy in the orange glow of the streetlights. I could hear the hum of traffic, the wailing of a faraway police car.

"What's your idea? Where do you want to go?" I asked.

"We'll catch the tube to Camden. I know this place."

My heart stopped. I didn't say anything.

"What?" she said.

"I can't get on a train, Rosa-Leigh."

She looked at me, and even though it was dark, I could see this light in her eyes. She *knew*. Someone must have told her. She said, "Sure you can," kind of slow.

I took a deep breath. I said, "I can't."

She waited.

"I just can't."

Rosa-Leigh said, "Let's do something else instead."

"I want to go home." I sounded like a whiny child, but I knew if I waited in the road another minute, I'd throw up. Suddenly my heart was beating madly and the cold was freezing the edges of my brain. I started hyperventilating.

She said, "Take a deep breath. You're all right. Just breathe." I could hear she was scared: her voice was higher than usual, tight. I sat on the curb and tears streamed down my face.

I said, "I'm dying," but it came out like a whisper.

She sat on the ground next to me and gave me a hug. And then she waited until I said I felt better. We got a cab to her house, where I stayed over.

SUNDAY, MARCH 26TH

When I got back from Rosa-Leigh's this morning, I clambered onto the roof. It was sunny and quite warm, so I curled up with a cup of tea and Fluffy, who deigned to sit next to me.

I remembered Mum, Emily, and me shopping together once in Soho. I must have been eight or nine. Mum walked ahead in shopping mode. Emily and I trailed behind, annoyed at having to keep up. The street was pretty, old buildings crowding along it like gossiping women and little boutique shops peeping out. I pointed out a shop to Emily. In the window was a beautiful golden globe. We looked at it for a moment, and then, without telling Mum, we went inside.

An old woman was sitting on a chair in the back of the room, her legs crossed and her hands folded in her lap. Emily said something to her, but the woman didn't answer. We took another step closer, and I knew, I just knew, something wasn't right. The woman's head was lowered and she was sitting very still.

I said Emily's name, but she didn't hear me or she couldn't believe what she was seeing, because she walked right up to the woman and put her hand on her shoulder. She pulled her hand away fast.

I looked at the old woman peacefully sitting there.

Emily whispered, "She's dead."

And then the old woman jerked her head up and her eyes sprang open. The pair of us screamed. We fled the shop and thundered down the street. Soon we were in narrow lanes that we didn't recognize. I started crying. I looked around and Emily wasn't there. I screamed, "Emily! Emily!"

Emily ran up to me and seized my hand. "Hey, hey, I'm here. Don't worry, I'm not going to leave you. I'm not going anywhere. I was just behind you."

"I didn't know where you were." I sobbed.

"It's okay."

"Was that woman dead? How did she come back to life?"

She had her arms around me. "It's okay. It's all okay." She sounded like Mum.

"Where are we?" I said.

"It'll be all right. Don't worry, Sophie."

"But where are we?"

Emily shushed me and put her arm tighter around my shoulders. She sat me on a bench. She said, "Don't worry. I'm not going to leave you. Mum will find us."

Mum came around the corner then, frantic. She grabbed hold of me and then of Emily. I'd forgotten that: she grabbed hold of me first.

"I've been out of my mind," she said.

"We got lost," Emily replied. "We thought this woman was dead. She can't have been, though." Looking back, I realize that the woman must have just been sleeping. The dead don't come back to life.

Mum squirreled her eyebrows together. "What woman? What are you talking about?"

I tried to say something, but I had a sudden urge to giggle. Now Mum was over being relieved, she started telling us off. I squeezed my sister's hand. Even as Mum was yelling, Emily whispered to me, "Told you it'd be all right."

But it's not all right. Not at all.

7

In a puddle of grey

MONDAY, MARCH 27TH

On my way to school I was making a long list of resolutions
like I should have made on New Year's. I resolved to go
jogging twice a week even if it was raining. To eat more
fruits and vegetables, and do a yoga DVD on Wednesdays
and Fridays. To lose a little weight—although not as much
as Abi has lost; she looked really thin today—and get toned
in the right places. I want to make sure all my underwear
matches, just in case I do ever have a boyfriend. (Not Dan,

though. I wish I would stop thinking about him.) I want to paint my nails and have them look nice. I want to write more poems and read a book every week. I want to go back to doing something like drama or judo, one of the things I used to do before everything fell apart. And I want to stick to the one resolution I did make on New Year's Day: to forget all about it, to move on.

As the morning slid by, I got more and more stressed. I ended up spending the afternoon in the bathroom. Eventually the bell rang for the end of school. I was shaking and hysterical. I watched out the window and saw Rosa-Leigh standing at the stone arch waiting for me, checking her watch. Then, when she'd gone, when everyone had gone and the janitor was about to lock up the building, I escaped and hurried through the park to get home.

When I'd calmed down, I looked on the internet to see if I could find out what was wrong with me. The only thing that fit my symptoms of nausea, mad heartbeat, crazy thoughts, difficulty breathing, and feeling frightened is "panic attacks," which sound like the sort of thing people get who are really messed up. I'm definitely not going to tell anyone about this; I don't want everyone to think I'm completely insane.

Trust me to get panic attacks, if that's what they are. I'm so lame. Everything's lame. Why can't I just get a grip? I called Rosa-Leigh, deciding that I needed to stop thinking about all of this. We chatted about what a bitch Abigail is being, and Rosa-Leigh moaned about how much homework she has. It was all very normal, and for a moment I forgot all the stuff about panic attacks. Rosa-Leigh said she has a surprise for me on Thursday and I totally have to come to her house. Thank God for her. If there even is a God.

THURSDAY, MARCH 30TH

I'm staying at Rosa-Leigh's tonight. I wonder what the surprise is. . . .

FRIDAY, MARCH 31ST

Last night was amazing! We got to Rosa-Leigh's, and all her family was there, including her dad. It's so fun to have a dad around, especially a dad like hers who is so friendly. He's short for a man but really broad-shouldered and red-faced, with a huge beard. Even he says he looks like a bear, which is the family joke. He told heaps of stories about Canada and made everyone laugh.

All her brothers were there, including Joshua, her oldest brother (I worked out which one is which) and who I SWEAR looked at me more than once and held my gaze until I blushed. He was sweet and funny and much better looking than Dan. (Although Dan has such nice eyes. But I have to forget about Dan, anyway.) Joshua even made sure I got enough spaghetti Bolognese, which Mum never makes anymore because we eat only takeaways or leftovers. I miss roast dinners and Mum's crazy health kicks. It's like now she can't even bear us sitting together to eat. Not that I ever want to sit and eat with her. Anyway, the spaghetti Bolognese was the best ever. Rosa-Leigh's dad made it.

After dinner Rosa-Leigh's dad dropped us off somewhere in Camden. She said, "There it is," pointing to a tattered red door. Above it hung a lamp, very nineteen-forties and cool. We pushed open the door, and it was like going into someone's house, all these sofas everywhere and beautiful lamps with colored glass that Rosa-Leigh said were Tiffany. I thought Tiffany was the jewelry shop in New York, but I didn't say anything. I sat on a sofa and looked at the crazy-haired people in the room, all dread-locks and braids, wearing multicolored jumpers and skirts. Stuff Emily would have thought was amazing. Except she wasn't there and I was.

The sofa smelled of dust and smoke. It was covered in a flower pattern. Rosa-Leigh smiled and said hi to a couple who were sitting at a nearby table. Then she went to get us drinks. She didn't get asked for ID like I would have been. I suddenly felt like I always want to feel: like I fit into my own life.

Rosa-Leigh brought us over gin and tonics. It's the sort of drink my mum would have. Rosa-Leigh said it was the sort of drink she thought everyone in England had all the time, which I told her it wasn't.

I asked her what this place is. She put her finger to her lips and raised an eyebrow in a *wait-and-see* gesture.

Then the lights went low, and over in one corner I saw the microphone in a spotlight. A black guy with the most gorgeous face went up to the mike. I could hardly stop looking at him, not because I fancied him but because he was so classically handsome that he looked like a painting. Then he started to talk. Except he wasn't talking; he was saying POEMS. He recited this most amazing poem about war and bombs. I shivered as if someone were kissing my neck (which made me fantasize about Dan). It felt like the guy was saying the poem for me. Except he wasn't saying it like it was a poem; he was saying it like it was REAL. I imagined Dan whispering along my spine.

After he was done, I clapped so hard my hands stung. Then a huge woman did three poems about sex and being a woman. She was hilarious. There were maybe four or five poets after that, all different stuff. One guy was no older than me, I swear. He looked like the sort of kid who sits at the front of class peering through his glasses. The sort of guy who is really awkward around girls. Except then he did this series of poems as fluid as water.

I asked Rosa-Leigh how she knew about this place. She leaned forward and whispered, "One of the exciting things about coming to London is spoken-word events like this."

I'd never heard of spoken-word events. I wondered

suddenly what Abigail would think of all this and saw the room through her eyes. She'd be trying to get the attention of all the other people there by speaking loudly and too much because she was uncomfortable.

Just then I caught my breath because I thought I saw Emily come into the room and sit at an empty table nearby. She scratched her neck and looked over at me. Except it wasn't her. It was someone who looked like her, that's all.

Rosa-Leigh must have seen my eyes get all wet because she squeezed my forearm and said, "You miss her, right?"

And I didn't ask her how she knew. I didn't have to.

SATURDAY, APRIL 1ST

April Fools' Day. I sat on the roof this morning remembering April Fools' Day last year. Emily called and said she was pregnant. Mum started screaming and yelling, and I came out of my room to see what all the fuss was about. I took the phone from Mum. Emily was laughing so hard, she could hardly speak.

"Don't tell her I'm joking: I told her I was pregnant," she said.

I started laughing, too, and Mum got even more mad before she realized what was going on. She didn't laugh, though. She didn't think joking about being pregnant was funny at all. I wonder now if we were happy then. Was that a good day?

It's not even lunchtime and today has already been too long. Mum and I are stuck in the house together. I finished reading a book by Stephen King; once I start reading one of his books, I can't put it down. Then I tried something Rosa-Leigh suggested. It's called a found poem. What you do is take words that you've found and put them together to make a poem. You "find" the words by choosing sentences, or bits of sentences, you really like. Then you rearrange them to make something new. It was something I thought Mum might like to do with me, but I didn't know how to ask her to join in. Things are not great between us. She was going out anyway.

"Where are you going?"

"Highgate, to the church. Do you want to come?"

I was amazed she asked me, but I couldn't stop myself saying no. I ignored Mum's sigh.

Here's my first attempt at the poem.

The reminder
Early Monday, Tuesday, Wednesday
For Emily
She was too late

It's short. I used one of Mum's magazines for it. I'm going to use a couple of books from the living room to try and make up a better poem.

He does teach the Bible
Has just written a book
He believes that his use of psychology
Is a hard-core Biblical message

Maybe I should have gone with Mum. I haven't been to the church yet this year. I last went on the day before Christmas. It only made me cry. At least Fluffy's here with me, purring and kneading my lap with her black paws. I stroked her and she tried to bite my hand, then jumped off and slunk away. I could tell by her catty disappointment that she finds me a poor substitute for Emily.

In the end I gave up on the poem and climbed onto the roof. I started thinking about this stupid fight Emily and I had about a year ago. I was watching TV when Emily walked into the room wearing a green skirt.

I said, "Where's your skirt from? It's nice."

"I cut it up from an old dress."

"What old dress?" My stomach sank.

"A green dress I found in the wardrobe."

"Whose wardrobe?"

"I don't know." The phone rang. She was already on her way out of the room.

I waited for her to finish talking to whoever it was, listening to her grating cheerful voice, each word sticking itself into my ears like a cotton bud pushed too far. When she got off the phone, I bounded from the sofa and grabbed a hold of the skirt. "What wardrobe?"

"Get off me! Get off!" she yelled.

"That's MY DRESS you've cut up! My favorite dress."

"It was too tight on you anyway."

I slapped her cheek and she reeled back. "You cow," she said. Even as she said it, I knew I'd gone too far, but I couldn't stop.

"What's your problem, Emily?" I screamed at her. "You can't bear something not to be yours. I loved that dress and you knew it."

"You looked like a tart in it."

"No, I didn't," I yelled. "You're just old and you can't wear a dress like that anymore."

She tried to get away, but I had her backed against the wall.

I screamed, "I didn't look like a tart in it! I looked totally great in it, which is why you had to cut it up. Right?"

"I don't know why you're so stressed out. It's better as a skirt. You can borrow it if you want."

I hated her at that moment. I wanted to slap her again, but I knew it wouldn't make me feel any better. I wanted to spit in her face. I said, "I wouldn't touch it if you paid me." Then I backed away and started crying.

"Come on," she said, "it's only a dress. I'll get you another one."

"I hate you."

"Take the stupid skirt. You can have it." She pulled it

down and stood in her white knickers in the corridor. I walked into the living room and turned up the TV insanely loud. My blood was pulsing in my body. I kept thinking about her face as I hit her, the red mark on her cheek, the way she stood in the corridor in her underwear holding out the skirt. I stayed sitting on the sofa with my arms crossed, waiting for the rage to die down.

Now I can't even believe I got angry about it. It seems so stupid.

MONDAY, APRIL 3RD

Mum came into my room just now. She sat on the edge of the bed and told me a friend of hers was coming over a week from Friday. She said she'd be really happy if I could be there. I could tell from her voice that she was nervous but also kind of excited. I remembered how she'd been going to that support group and how she had tried to talk to me a couple of times recently. And now here she was sitting on the end of my bed smiling. What was going on with her? I lay there and flung my arm over my eyes.

She said, "Are you all right?"

"I didn't think you'd even noticed."

"That's not fair, Sophie."

"What's fair about life, Mum?" I said. I squeezed back the tears that were fizzing up.

I thought for a moment she was going to put her hand on

my shoulder and I thought for a moment she was going to make it all better so I could say to her, "I miss you."

Except she said, "I don't know what to do, Sophie. I really am trying. I know it's not good enough. I know I haven't been doing very well."

Even though you'd think what she'd said would have made me feel better, it didn't. It was like I went crazy. Like the right numbers had been rolled into the combination lock and I was opened up. I sat suddenly and yelled at her to get out. I told her I didn't want to meet her stupid friend and I was sick of us pretending. Mum's face went slack. The light faded from her eyes. I hadn't realized until it was gone that she'd had light there because it's been so long since she's looked happy. I'd just made her miserable again. I couldn't stop though; I yelled, "You don't care about me!"

"I'm sorry, Sophie," she said. "I'm doing my best. I promise. I've been going to a support group to try and get myself together. I know how hard this is—"

"You never have time for me. You never even see me. And now you have a friend coming over and everything is supposed to be FINE?" I could hear how horrible I was being. And then I caught her look. I said, "Your friend is a man, right?" Even as I said it, I was hoping she'd tell me I was wrong.

She looked down and then looked back up at me, tears in her eyes. She said, "Please, Sophie. He's just a friend. And

I have been trying, I have, but I don't know how to make this better."

What was I supposed to say to that? *I* couldn't make things better. It was *my* fault in the first place. It was my stupid shoelace. I was on the far side of the bed from her and tears leaked out of me. I said, "You have no idea what it was like. No one has any idea what I live with EVERY day." Then I started screaming, "Get out! Get out!" I told her again and again to get out, but I stopped yelling it. My voice became quieter and stiffer. I repeated the words, frightening myself. She gave me the saddest look, but she left. I took a deep breath. Fear clambered over me like a body trying to get out of a grave. My heart slammed, my breathing became choked, I cried silent tears. I got into bed and lay there shaking. I thought I was going to die.

TUESDAY, APRIL 4TH

I pretended I was going to school this morning. I've never done this before, but I was feeling too shaky and weird to go in. I left without speaking to Mum. I waited on the other side of the road from our house, not knowing what I was doing. It was warm, and little yellow flowers are poking through the scratches of earth by the straggly trees on our road. I could smell blossoms and hear birds singing. I was dizzy with panic, and I wasn't really sure what I planned to do with the day. Luckily Mum came out after a while.

I wondered where she was going, but when I got inside, there was a note in case she got back later than me saying she planned to go food shopping and clothes shopping and then over to Highgate church.

Indoors, I shut out the liveliness of spring. I thought it would be really quiet, but houses without people in them aren't quiet; they're more creaking and breathy, like they have personalities of their own. I wondered what sort of personality our house has—sort of melancholy and lost, I'd think. The wooden floor varnished by Mum creaked as I brushed past the dresser with the old phone on it (so old it has a dial). The mirror reflected me walking past, and I was shocked at my pale, wrecked appearance. I fingered the big dark circles under my eyes. The hanging plants over the door to the living room needed watering, but I didn't get the watering can. Instead I stood looking at all the books in there, the paintings on the wall that Mum did years ago. I tried to recall when it was that she gave up painting. I remembered then that she used to play the saxophone when I was little; she used to play and Emily and I would mock her and beg her to stop. And she did stop at some point. I couldn't remember when I'd last heard her play. If I'd known it was the last time, I'd have begged her to play on.

I climbed the stairs. I stopped at Emily's door, pushed it open, looked at her things laid out like they always had been. I fell to my knees, this sound coming out of me:

the howl of a wounded animal. I clutched my stomach and doubled over. The pain did not go away. I could not stop crying.

WEDNESDAY, APRIL 5TH

Ms. Bloxam, all sweaty with her hair falling around her chubby face, lumbered up to me at break today and said OUT OF THE BLUE, "How are you dealing with the whole thing?"

She said "the whole thing" like it was a *thing* under the bed. Weird word *thing*. All words are weird if you keep using them too much. *Weird* is a weird word.

Considering Ms. Bloxam usually looks like she's about to have a heart attack and has a bulgy, googly-eyed thing going on, she actually looked SO sympathetic, I couldn't believe it. I felt like crying and then I felt like running out of the room or throwing up, but I just stood there and nodded.

She said, "Are you *okay*?" She has really long red nails that she must spend ages on every few days, maybe even paying for manicures, despite the fact the rest of her looks swollen and awful. Her expensive perfume wafted over me. I looked at her fingernails and then back up at her face, thinking I was going to tell her that I wasn't okay, not really.

She was glancing at the clock. She was obviously too

busy to hear how I really felt. I said, "I'm fine."

She nodded and said, "You're doing well." Then she went out of the room, and I stood there, shaking. I went into the bathroom and tried to calm down. I thought I was going to throw up but I didn't in the end.

I could imagine Ms. Bloxam in the staff room having a cup of tea and a doughnut, thinking she'd been good to me and feeling all pleased with herself. But she didn't do anything, not really. Then I felt bad for having such mean thoughts; she'd only been trying.

THURSDAY, APRIL 6TH

Oh my God. Lucy Haywood's dad, Mark, had a heart attack. He was playing squash, and he just keeled over. Mum and I are going to the hospital now to see if he's okay. He's not dead but it sounds pretty bad. If I was sure there was a God, I'd have this to say to Him right now: "STOP MESSING EVERYTHING UP FOR EVERYONE!"

Mum let me miss school—she didn't know it was the second time this week—and spend the day at the hospital. Normally she wouldn't, but—and she said this—considering everything that's happened to us and how supportive the Haywoods have been, we might want to be there for them. This morning the doctors really thought Mark wouldn't make it, and then there was a long operation. We spent all day bringing them tea. Mum held Katherine's hand.

Mum was so supportive and nice. Like a mum. And we didn't mention the most recent fight we'd had or anything. I brought her two cups of coffee, and she smiled and said, "Thank you," and she looked like herself. Then FINALLY the doctor came out and said Katherine and Lucy and the twins could go and see Mark. Mum stepped back and— no one saw except me—she had this look on her face like someone had put something sharp against her throat: she winced. I wasn't sure if she was happy or sad. The worst thing is that I knew exactly how she felt.

Katherine and everyone went into Mark's room. Mum and I sat in the corridor in *total* silence. Horrible. Then Lucy came out a while later and said her dad was talking, and she was all excited. She went straight back in. It was pretty obvious we didn't need to be there anymore. I thought about them all in the room together as a family, and I felt like Mum and I were the loneliest people on the planet.

If something bad had happened to them, like if Mark had become worse, then we might not have felt so lonely at the hospital. But then Mark would be dead, which would be awful. God, I don't even know what I'm trying to write.

I was thinking in the car on the way home about a family holiday we all took. It must have been ten years ago, because I was really young. I think it was the year we went to France. But anyway, we were by a lake, and it was really hot. Mark and Katherine are there in the memory with Lucy and the baby twins, obviously. Mark is throwing a ball up and catching it. I can see the ball, a red ball, against the blue sky, just hanging there for that extra beat before it starts to fall to Mark's waiting hands.

I do want him to get better. I want him to get out of the hospital.

8

Last summer lies

School. Horrible. When I walked through the main doors, my heart was beating so fast it scared me. I spent all of morning break feeling panicky. Rosa-Leigh was away sick. Megan and Abigail were doing some project together, so they weren't around. I ended up having to talk to Zara, and neither of us could think of anything to say, so I told her all about Mark's heart attack. She tried really hard to look interested.

Then, during lunch break, ABIGAIL came over to me.

I could tell she was standing next to me even without looking up. She coughed and said, "Hey, how are you?"

"Why do you care?"

"Because we're friends."

I looked straight at her, completely confused. After the fight we had, I didn't think we'd ever make up. I'm not sure I even want to be friends with her anyway. She wasn't looking straight back at me, more off to one side, and she shifted foot to foot.

She said, "I heard about Mark Haywood from Zara. It's really sad. How's he doing?" She knows the Haywoods because she's met them at our house before.

I suddenly realized she was only coming to make up because she felt bad for me. A sympathy apology, not a real one. I've never felt so distant from her—even when we were screaming at each other it wasn't this bad.

I said, "He's fine. You don't have to worry." I couldn't help remembering all the horrible things she'd said when we fought, and how she read out my apology letter, and how she flung herself at Dan.

"Good. I'm glad," she said.

"Yeah, everything's fine."

She leaned over suddenly and gave me a hug like everything was okay. She felt really bony, a bit like a bird. She asked me to come and sit with everyone, which I did, then she started to go on about her and Dan. I got all shaky because I hated her so much again, even though she doesn't know I like him. I made my excuses, which Abigail hardly noticed, she was so wrapped up in *Dan this, Dan that*, and left the table to wander outside on my own. I know I haven't heard from Dan in ages and he's seeing Abigail and I should just get over him, but there is just something there I can't stop thinking about. I'm an idiot.

Because it was sunny all day, I thought the winter might have finally melted away, but as I was leaving school, it got really cold and I half froze to death waiting for the bus. When I got home, I wrote a prose poem about the word *death*. I guess that was the mood I was in.

> **Death**—*inky blue, she gives in to you, she takes you home and away from home and in the dark tunnel there she waits, lonely hot, like fire, like waste, like the sticky smell of rubbish in the heat and there's no end to her waiting, her patience, her simple, easy smile, and she takes your hand and leads you away from me and I can't stop her, not this death, not this woman waiting in the darkness like a dancer with veils, revealing nothing, she takes you slowly and then faster, and the ache of death is nothing compared to the smell of rubbish in the heat.*

SUNDAY, APRIL 9TH

The weekend slid by like mud.

The Haywoods called early this morning to tell us that Mark is doing much better. He might even get to go home soon. I felt lots calmer when I heard. At lunch at school everyone was in the cafeteria because it was raining. Abigail was being okay, although things are still weird between us. Zara was making everyone laugh. Even Megan wasn't being too bad. Kalila was sitting with us, and we were all talking and it was really cool for once.

Megan suggested we play a game. She said we should each take a sheet of paper and write our name along the top. Our name would be passed around and everyone else could write whatever she wanted about that person. Secretly.

No one really wanted to do it, but we were curious, too—you could tell because everyone sat a little straighter, leaning forward. Abigail wrote down her name, then handed her sheet to Megan and said, "Let's do it. There's nothing else to do."

I wrote my name, so did Kalila, Yasmin, and Zara. Rosa-Leigh jumped up and went to sit with some other girls. I wish now that I'd done the same thing.

Abigail said, "Get writing," to everyone. I wrote on Abigail's that she could be the most amazing person but she's very unpredictable and could be mean when she didn't even realize it. And bossy.

Here's what everyone wrote about me, and before the

116

statement, who I think wrote it. The list makes me feel
HORRIBLE.

Yasmin: I like Sophie, but sometimes she's a bit emotional, which is under-
standable but hard to deal with.

Zara: She is clever and sweet but quite clingy.

Kalila: She is funny and lively and good at English. She is
perhaps too easily led by everyone else's opinions. She
gets sad sometimes. I'd like to know her better.

Abigail (and this is the WORST): Sophie thinks she's better than
everyone. She thinks she's the most intelligent person in the world and also that she
knows more about real life than everyone else. She's judgmental. She is self-obsessed,
and she cries too much. She's much more uptight than she used to be, which I know
isn't her fault. When she isn't in a bad mood, she's good fun to be with.

Megan: I think she's a bit boring but all right. She never wants to do
fun stuff and gets all worried when the rest of us do. She's hard to get
along with and VERY moody. Emotional roller-coaster!

The bell rang. I sat with the words from that sheet of paper
burning a hole in my head all afternoon. Rosa-Leigh wasn't
very sympathetic when I told her on the bus that I was
really hurt by some of the things that people wrote. She
said, "Don't ever ask someone else what they think of you.

117

You'll never hear what you want to hear."

I said, "How would you know?"

"It's just how it is." She told me to tear up the sheet of paper and forget about it.

The whole thing makes me wonder how it is that I can see myself one way and everyone else can see something else. I NEVER thought I was judgmental. And I don't really think of myself as too emotional, or at least I didn't. I think I've had a lot of bad stuff happen recently. When Emily was around, I was different, I'm sure. Happier. I wish I hadn't played the stupid game.

TUESDAY, APRIL 11TH

I can't face going to school. I have to go: we have a big talk today about our future. I always tune out of those sorts of talks. As if I care about the future. As if any of that matters. It's the last day of term before the Easter holiday, but I just can't face it.

I told Mum I was too sick to go in. It wasn't true, but she didn't even question me. She shrugged and said she'd make me scrambled eggs on toast, which she brought to me with tomatoes cut up, how I like them. I was amazed she remembered. She pottered around downstairs and didn't seem to mind that I watched TV nearly all day. A couple of times she looked like she might come and sit next to me, but I glared at her, so she stayed away. I thought about writing a poem, but there were no words in my head.

Rosa-Leigh just called to see if I was okay. I told her I had the flu. We chatted for a bit, and I found myself complaining about Mum wanting me to meet her guy friend, even though, since our fight and Mark's heart attack, there's been no mention again of him coming around. I guess it's been on my mind. Rosa-Leigh went very quiet.

"What? I can't handle Mum doing this to me," I said.

"Well, what if your mom needs a friend right now?" Rosa-Leigh said softly, like she didn't want to upset me but she couldn't stop herself asking.

"What about me?" I said, hearing that I was being selfish.

"Maybe she needs someone to help her through."

"I don't think you should defend her."

There was an awkward pause. "Okay," said Rosa-Leigh. Then she changed the subject. She said, "Abigail asked me to her place for that party on Friday."

"Another party?"

She said, "Want to come with me?"

"I can't," I lied. "My mum's calling; I have to go." I got off the phone feeling weird. I could totally go to the party. I haven't got anything to do on Friday. But Abigail hasn't asked me, even though we're supposed to be friends again.

Sometimes I wish I were a thousand miles away.

Somewhere different. With a different life and a different mum and a family like the Haywoods or Rosa-Leigh's family. I'm going to have a shower and NOT THINK ABOUT ANY OF THIS EVER AGAIN.

WEDNESDAY, APRIL 12TH

I sat on the roof tonight, listening to the radio. It was warm enough that I needed only a thin jumper. Spring has eroded winter, and soon it will be summer. Sitting up there, I found it wasn't long before I thought about summer last year. I thought about the night Emily eventually got home for the summer.

I remembered Mum and I had been waiting for hours. We sat watching day turn into darkness, pretending to be interested in the TV. At one point Mum said, "Sophie, stop drumming your fingers on the table." A bit later she said, "Surely you should have something better to do," but she was being grumpy only because Emily was late.

I watched out the window. After a while I went to get a book. Mum asked me what I was reading, and she seemed like she genuinely wanted to know, but I ignored her. When Emily did arrive, we flung ourselves into her arms, and we were so busy hugging her and helping her with her bags and putting dinner back on the table, that the long wait was almost forgotten.

Afterward I wished I could have every minute of that long evening all over again. Waiting for Emily was so much better, it turned out, than not waiting for her.

Emily kicked off her red slip-on shoes. She pulled her hair into a ponytail, showing off moonstone earrings. Her dress, funky and short, had red and silver swirls all over. I looked down at my own jeans. I could never wear a dress like that. Emily stroked Fluffy, who purred with delight, then swept into the kitchen to her plate of food.

We sat with her while she talked about her courses and this job she'd been doing since her classes finished: helping people in the community paint and draw their painful experiences. She always had jobs where she did good things for others: working at an old people's home when she was younger, spending some of her weekends volunteering at a center for learning-disabled kids. I'd seen Emily stop in the street to give a homeless person a sandwich she'd bought for herself.

I watched her talking, her mouth moving quickly, her hands leaping. She told us that she had a new boyfriend, and I wondered if I'd met him. I'd gone to Leeds twice to stay in her house there: a huge place full of people who had colorful bedrooms and who always seemed to be coming in or going out. One of them wanted to be a pilot; another wanted to work in TV. I wondered if her new boyfriend was the guy who'd had the downstairs bedroom—a well-built, classically good-looking guy who'd stared at Emily every time she spoke.

As soon as Emily had finished—she ate only half the pasta and none of the salad because she was talking so much,

121

twirling her fork and then pushing the plate to one side—she went to get something to show us. She came back to the kitchen with a large rucksack and opened it ceremoniously on the cork floor. She pulled a couple of ordinary tree branches—well, more like large twigs—from inside and set them on the table. I picked up her plate, scraped the remains into the bin, and put the plate in the dishwasher. Mum made us all a cup of tea. Emily told us that the branches were going to be a family tree—a project she was making. From each branch she would hang the faces of our family printed onto leaves.

Mum told us she had an old album with a family tree inscribed on the front page. She went to get it. While she was gone, Emily winked at me and put her hand on my forearm. She asked me how I was.

"Fine. Happy it's summer," I said. I wanted to say so many things, but I was suddenly shy of her because we hadn't spoken that much while she was at Leeds. I looked away and then back, willing myself to talk.

She leaned forward to say something, but then her mobile rang, and she stopped whatever she was saying to answer it. She spoke softly. I listened, trying to work out who it was. Her voice sounded lighter when she talked to her friends than when she talked to us. She sounded like a stranger. She got off the phone and sat back down. I thought now would be the chance to chat with her alone, but Mum came in and the moment was lost.

Mum was showing Emily the names of long dead family members. I looked out the window and wished there were stars to count. The light pollution in London meant I could rarely see stars. Light pollution and clouds. I felt suddenly lonely and tuned back into the conversation. Emily wondered if withered leaves could represent the dead, like Dad. It seemed morbid to me.

Mum switched off the lamps and lit the candles. I watched the little flames dance. It was nice having Emily home. I had missed all the noise and excitement and drama she brought, the quiet winks she sent in my direction when Mum gave me a hard time, the way she knew me better than anyone in the world did.

Emily and Mum talked on. I watched the candles burning low, the shapes made by the shadows. As the last flame began to flicker, Mum told us it was time for bed.

Emily agreed with her. She was tired; she'd been out late the night before with friends. I was jealous of those people who got to spend time with her instead of me. And disappointed. I wanted to carry on talking to my big sister alone. Mum offered us hot chocolate. She normally never had time to make me hot chocolate, and now I almost said no out of spite but I didn't. Mum made us a cup each, and I took mine to bed. I heard Emily answer her mobile in the room next to me and chatter away to someone deep into the night. I fell asleep to the sound of her voice.

I wish I could hear it again.

I woke in the middle of the night and I could hear Emily. I could HEAR her. It was as if she were sitting on my bed whispering in my ear. And she said, "Why did this happen? It's not fair." And she said it over and over until I put my hands over my ears and couldn't hear her anymore. Oh God, I feel like I'm falling from a great height and no one can catch me.

THURSDAY, APRIL 13TH

Rosa-Leigh called just now and was asking how I was. I didn't really want to talk to her, but she said straightaway, "I know you're mad about what I said about your mum's friend."

"I'm not mad."

"Well, I'm sorry."

"I just can't think about her now."

"That's fine, then. And I know you're mad about Abigail's thing. I only said I'd go because I thought you'd go with me."

"She hasn't even asked me."

"So what? It'll be fun."

I pulled a face and then happened to catch a glimpse of myself in the mirror, sitting on my bed feeling sorry for myself. I started to giggle. Rosa-Leigh started giggling down the phone line, too. She said, "I'll pick you up on the way there."

"You could come over first," I said. "We can catch the bus."

"I thought you were never going to ask me over."

"My house is not the most pleasant . . ."

There was a moment's silence and then Rosa-Leigh said, "My brother thinks you're cute."

"Which brother?" I blushed.

"Joshua. But you cannot date my brother."

"He really thinks I'm cute?"

"You cannot date my brother." She was laughing.

I said, "What time are you coming over?"

"Tomorrow afternoon?"

I somehow have to make my house a better place to be by then. Perhaps I can pretend Mum's not even in, so Rosa-Leigh doesn't have to meet her properly. Things are so tense and unpredictable between me and Mum, and I know a lot of it might be my fault, but I just can't handle being around her right now.

FRIDAY, APRIL 14TH

Rosa-Leigh arrived and we stayed in my room. I didn't go and tell Mum she was here or introduce them, even though I knew I probably should. Rosa-Leigh and I were sitting on my bed and talking and laughing when there was a knock at my door and it swung open. Mum stood there looking as full of hope as a child at Christmas. She stared at Rosa-Leigh sitting on the bed.

She said, "You girls sound like you're having fun." She looked over at me, and she was so pleased, it was pathetic.

Rosa-Leigh got up and said, "I'm Rosa-Leigh. We met at my house the other week. Nice to see you again."

"Hello," Mum said. "Good to meet you. . . . Would you girls like something to eat?"

"We're all right, Mum," I said. I wanted her to go away and stop being so embarrassing.

"No. Let me make you something."

"We're fine. We're going to Abigail's."

"How's Abigail?" she said, and she smiled this fond smile. I thought she was going to come and sit down on the bed. I stood up and said, "We've got to get ready."

She said, "Let me give you a lift there."

I paused.

Rosa-Leigh said, "That would be great, thanks."

"We need to get ready now," I said.

Then Mum looked at me and, like a slow moon rising, comprehension shone from her face: she knew I didn't want her there. She said she'd be ready when we were and left.

I felt bad. I took a slow breath. I said, "Sorry about her."

Rosa-Leigh shrugged and said, "She's really nice. You should—" She stopped herself from saying anything else, and I was grateful.

* * *

126

Mum drove us to Abigail's. When Abigail opened the door, she looked terrible, really thin and pale. I said, "Hi." I wanted to ask her why she hadn't asked me to the party herself now we were supposed to be friends again, but I just smiled like nothing was wrong.

She looked as if she momentarily didn't recognize me, then with a big smile said, "Hi" back.

I was suddenly glad I'd come. I needed to talk to Abigail. I needed to make up with her properly. She is my best friend and I miss her. We used to have such a great time together, her coming up with wild ideas and me listening and laughing along. I thought for a moment she might hug me, but someone jostled past. Dan appeared and put his arms around her waist. I wondered what it would be like to have him enveloping me like that. I looked at Abigail's face, expecting to see her smiling. Her jaw was clenched. Even though she seemed uncomfortable with Dan, I was jealous. I wanted to be held like that.

I felt suddenly like there was a hedge between Abi and me. Not a wall—that would be too solid—but a hedge with thick, leafy branches. I could still see my best friend through the gaps between the leaves but I couldn't touch her.

Dan smiled at me then, and my body gave a little jolt, which I wished it hadn't, and I blushed. He's so sexy and his eyes are stunning. God, I really like him.

We went inside and got drinks. It was weird because

there were loads of people there I didn't know, whereas once Abi and I together would have phoned everyone to invite them. Who were all these people?

Megan was talking really loudly in the middle of the room and she was obviously already drunk. I talked to Zara for a bit, even though I remembered that during that stupid game she wrote I'm clingy. I tried to be cool and not clingy—even though I'm not clingy at all. Then I started wondering if it even had been Zara who wrote that. Fortunately her phone rang so I didn't have to think about it anymore.

I wandered over and sat and talked for a bit with this boy sitting next to me who was not cute AT ALL. I felt a bit sorry for him.

It was late by then. Everything was dark, and the house was full of people. For a moment I pictured more and more people pouring into the room, looming and fading in a crazy crush of bodies. It would be so easy to be trampled to death in a dark, crowded room. I imagined lying on the floor, blood pouring out of me, my limbs at strange angles, my lungs struggling to get air in after someone had accidentally stamped on me. I took a deep breath, made my mind change the subject. I wondered where Abigail's mum was. I'd never really seen the house like this; it felt like a house of strangers, not a house I'd spent so much time in, not a house I knew so well I could walk around it with my eyes closed.

I wanted to go to the bathroom, but the downstairs one was being used. I slipped upstairs, although Abigail had been putting all the coats on the steps to try to stop people going up there. The upstairs corridor was dark. I tiptoed along, remembering how even last year this house felt like my own home. Then, out of the dark, someone put his hand on my wrist.

I jumped.

A voice said, "Sorry, I didn't mean to scare you."

"Dan?" I spluttered. "What are you doing up here?"

"I just wanted to get away." He was standing in the doorway to Abi's room. His fingers were a bracelet around my wrist.

"Where's Abigail?"

He shrugged. "Come and talk to me a moment."

"I don't think so."

"No, I mean it, Sophie. I want to get to know you better."

"You and Abigail," I said, feeling nothing but the warmth of his hand.

"She's not up here, is she?" he said.

"I'm going back downstairs." I was saying it, but my stomach was fluttering with pleasure.

He bent closer, and a little light played on his face so I could see his eyes. I could smell his aftershave. "Don't be like that," he said.

"I should go."

"Don't go." He held my wrist tighter: a manacle.

"Dan," I said, and I didn't recognize my own voice.

He kissed me then, and I was so surprised— No, I'm lying. I knew he was about to kiss me. I wasn't surprised at all. And my mouth opened. I thought how easy it was for everything to change. How easy it was for me to change. Then I pushed against him. He slid his hand up into my hair. My skin tingled. I didn't want him to stop. I managed to pull away.

I said, "I can't do this to Abigail." I looked at him. My body shuddered. "I'm going now," I said.

"Stay." He leaned forward.

"I can't do this to her."

He lowered his head and kissed me again. His mouth was warm and his lips soft. I couldn't stop myself kissing him back. He ran his hand along my spine, lower. I tangled my hands in his hair and pressed against him. And then, just as he started to slip a hand under my top, I thought of Abigail, the shock on her face if she knew. I stepped back, my hands on his chest to steady myself. I didn't let myself look at him.

He said, "Sophie," but I turned from him and ran downstairs, nearly falling on the way down.

I sat next to Rosa-Leigh, who gave me a beer. She was talking with these two guys. And it was as if nothing had happened. Except my face was hot and I kept looking up to see if Dan was coming into the room. I thought about him upstairs in the dark.

I'm ashamed to say, after about five minutes, I figured he must still be waiting and I decided to go back to him, but just as I got up, Rosa-Leigh said we should go home. It felt like a sign or something, so I followed her out of the house, looking around one last time for Dan. I didn't say much to her in the cab so she asked if I was okay.

"I'm just tired," I said.

"I'm really sorry about what I said about your mum and her friend—it has nothing to do with me."

"I wasn't even thinking about it." And it was true; I wasn't thinking about Mum or Emily or anything. Then suddenly I wished Emily were in the car with me, that she were the one asking me if I was okay. I'd tell her all about Dan. She'd tell me what to do. I had to look away from Rosa-Leigh so she didn't see the tears fill my eyes. I swallowed them back.

My head is STILL SPINNING. I can't believe I kissed the guy my best friend's with, even if she isn't really my best friend anymore. But kissing him made me feel so good. It made me think about him and how he tasted and how he touched me, and for a moment I really did forget everything else. The worst of it is I want to kiss him again.

131

9

Where nothing can swim

Mum was out. Katherine called. Mark's definitely much better from his heart attack, although he's a bit quiet. I could hardly concentrate on anything she said; twice she asked if I was all right. All I could think about was Dan, and his intense blue eyes. I pretty much thought about Dan all day. Rosa-Leigh emailed me a poem by E. E. Cummings, who doesn't like capital letters and punctuation. I'm not sure about someone who doesn't use capital letters. I don't know; I'm weird like that: I like sentences to look neat. I'd never tell anyone that at school, not in a million years, but it's true. Anyway, I read the poem, and I *swear* it's about me and Dan. Here's the end of the poem.

> . . . *but*
> *i should rather than anything*
> *have(almost when hugeness will shut*
> *quietly)almost,*
> *your kiss*

I had to read it more than once. It's true about hugeness shutting quietly. Kissing Dan was the only time I haven't thought about Emily in forever. And I know I should feel bad about that but I don't.

SUNDAY, APRIL 16TH

I got up for breakfast, and Mum had put all these chocolate eggs out on the table. She'd made scrambled eggs and bacon. She smiled at me. I hardly looked at her. I made myself a cup of tea.

When I sat, she said, "Happy Easter."

I didn't reply.

She said, "We need to talk, Sophie."

I couldn't do it. I couldn't talk to her. Rage filled me up like I was a hot-air balloon about to burst. What's wrong with me? Why can't I sit and have a nice breakfast with Mum? I got up and walked out. I didn't want her to see me start crying. She called after me, but I slammed the door to my room and sat against it so she couldn't get in. She tried to shove it open, and she banged on the wood a couple of times. Then she said, "I love you. You know that, right?"

I didn't answer.

She said, "What should I do?"

But I'm not supposed to know the answer to that question. She is. But she doesn't because she still hasn't gone back to work or got her life together or anything. I reached for my iPod and jammed the headphones in my ears, turning the volume up high.

TUESDAY, APRIL 18TH

Dan hasn't called. And I forgot to see Lynda today. I only remembered when Rosa-Leigh and I were on our way to go shopping and I got this feeling like I'd left something behind. I couldn't for the life of me remember what I'd forgotten, and then I just had this sinking feeling like a ship was foundering in my stomach. Rosa-Leigh asked if I was okay. I didn't tell her where I was supposed to be; I just changed the subject, which was hard because my mind was full of Dan and now full of Lynda. Lynda would have wondered where I was. Not that we ever have anything to talk about. I haven't told her anything, really, nothing about the panic attacks, nothing about the past, but we keep up the charade.

I'd like to hear from DAN. I don't know if I should email him or call his mobile or wait for him to call me or what. Maybe kissing didn't even mean anything to him, but the way he'd looked at me, I SWEAR I COULD SEE INSIDE HIM. I swear with that look he was saying to me that he'd made a mistake with Abigail and that he wanted to be with me. And being with him would be so great. He's so cute and kind and such a good kisser. I can't believe how much I like him. I wish he'd call.

Mum was humming today. I heard her in the corridor. I stuck my head out of my room. She stopped and looked guilty, but then she smiled, all tired and weary looking, and started humming again. I smiled back. Just quickly.

WEDNESDAY, APRIL 19TH

Mum just came into my room. Apparently, Lynda called about me forgetting our appointment and I have to go and see her tomorrow. Why isn't Lynda on her Easter HOLIDAY?

Mum asked, "Why didn't you go?"

I just shrugged.

Mum sighed and said, "Sophie," and her voice was gentle.

"What?"

"You have to talk to me."

"I just forgot to go, all right? There's nothing to say."

"What about how we're getting on? Why couldn't you have Easter breakfast with me? We need to talk about that."

"I don't want to talk. I don't want to think. I don't want to remember."

"I know, sweetheart."

"No, you don't. You don't know because you weren't there. You have no idea what it's like, what I see in my head when I close my eyes. Sometimes I'll be in a room, like at a party, and I'll imagine everyone in there being crushed to death."

She pressed her mouth together as if she were physically hurt for me. She said softly, "Tell me more. I want to be here for you."

"It happens when I least expect it; these images come into my head. I don't WANT to go into it. It's never going to get better, and there's nothing you can do. If I hadn't had to tie up my STUPID SHOELACE, everything would be different. Don't you understand it's my fault?"

"Of course it's not."

"What do you know? You act like you're over it, but you haven't gone back to work even though you're making me go to school. I can't deal with it."

"I am going back to work."

"When?"

"Monday."

"Why didn't you tell me?"

"I'm telling you now." Mum folded her arms across her chest. "You haven't been very easy to talk to." She said it softly, as if she was being kind, but that just bothered me more.

I took a step back. I tried not to yell, but the words came out loudly. "*I* haven't been easy to talk to. What about *you*?"

"Sophie," she said again.

"You always had time for her. You never had time for me. It's because you were the same—she was just like you. I'm different and awkward and nothing like her. You don't want to make time for me. You just want her back."

"Let's not start screaming at each other," she said steadily. "We have to make room for dialogue."

"You're not my stupid therapist, and you have NO IDEA WHAT YOU'RE TALKING ABOUT."

She stepped forward and I stepped neatly around her. She said, "I'm sorry I didn't tell you I was going back to work. The doctor finished my compassionate leave a while ago, and I don't want to use all of your father's life insurance to keep us going. That money's for you." She spoke calmly and slowly.

"I don't care that you're going back to work."

She said, "And I never want you to compare yourself to her."

137

"You can't even say her name," I hissed, and backed up to my bedroom door. "I'm going out," I said.

"We need to talk."

"Stop all the stupid *make room for dialogue* crap and leave me alone." I fled from my room and flew down the stairs and out the front door before she could say anything else.

I ran up the road until I reached the high street, where cars roared, beeping at one another. A group of people tumbled out of a café into the dusk. The orange interior light spilled over the street. I imagined the flames of a huge fire flaring from the open door, people fleeing—the men coughing and dribbling with fear; the women, their eyes wide as those of dead fish, stumbling blindly in the smoke; the wail of ambulances. I leaned against a wall and took several deep breaths.

Mum is going back to work. She's over it. I should have been pleased, but anger surged inside me like lava in a volcano. She's good at her job—our house is evidence of how good; everyone used to say how beautiful it is inside. Everyone being our family friends, friends who don't come around anymore. Not that they didn't try to come around after the funeral.

THURSDAY, APRIL 20TH

When I sat down for my rescheduled appointment with Lynda she asked me repeatedly if I was okay. She wanted

138

to know why I'd forgotten to go last time. I ignored her. Each visit, it gets easier to sit in silence, pretending she's not even there.

She wanted to talk to me about Dad today. I didn't have anything to say about him; I was so little when he died. I thought instead about Mark Haywood. I remembered Mark drinking too much one night and deciding to go swimming in the lake near their house. It was dark outside. Mum and Katherine were telling him not to be so stupid, that he'd freeze to death. Mark swam across the whole lake. When he came back in, he was shivering cold but he was FULL OF LIFE. Not dead, nowhere near it.

Mark continues to get much better from his heart attack, although apparently he's very shaken. Adults say that a lot: "shaken." It doesn't seem the right word to me to describe how you feel after something bad's happened. Shaken is how you feel when you've been on a roller-coaster, all lively and buzzing. Shaken is how Mark felt when he swam in the lake that night, I'm sure. I could see in his eyes how he was all shaken up inside, happy, excited. When something bad's happened, you feel numb, like it's not real. You feel dead on the inside. Not shaken at all.

I had a nap and dreamed that huge hands tore up a photograph of Emily, Mum, and me strip by strip. It was a heart-stopping dream. I woke up sweating and tiptoed to

Mum's collection room and opened the door. There was even more stuff in there than last time, but I wasn't looking at her stuff. I was looking for the photographs. I found our birth certificates in the desk, along with all our passports and legal documents. The passport picture of Emily made me swell with tears. I tried to remember where Mum keeps the photo albums.

I riffled through the shelves. I didn't feel calm anymore or sad; instead I was panicky and disorganized. My breath was ragged. I didn't know exactly what I was looking for. It was like I'd gone crazy. I pulled down all these gloves and scarves and a beautiful gold necklace with a red stone surrounded by silver petals. I shuffled through a little pile of papers that turned out to be letters that Mum must have found lying around over the years.

Then I saw an album beneath. It was full of photographs of me and Emily. I started crying. I took the album with me as I left the room, hurried to the bathroom, and slipped out the window onto the roof. I looked at the photos until my heart felt like a badly bruised apple.

At the back of the album is a photograph of us outside the house we lived in when I was really little. I touched the photograph. Mum is standing in the middle holding me in her arms, and Emily is on her right. Emily is wearing red plastic boots and is waving at the camera. I wonder if Dad was taking the picture—he died when I was two, and in the photograph I'm only a baby. I'm smiling up at

Mum. I turned the photograph over. On the back it says *18 Bowood Road* in Mum's handwriting.

Suddenly I felt like I know why she keeps lost things in her collection. And I felt like I wanted to go to our old house on Bowood Road and be back in that place where everything was still good. All I wanted to do was go back. Back to the moments before it happened when everything was okay.

Sitting on the roof makes me feel calmer. It gives me a view of the world below, lets me take a breath. I stroked Emily's cheek in the picture. She was so happy.

I remembered that morning last summer. It feels so long ago, yet it's all terribly clear in my head. I woke really early. *Emily is home for the rest of the summer.* The thought popped in my mind, and I launched myself out of bed and into her room. She wasn't there. I went into the kitchen, and she was sitting at the breakfast table.

"Hi," I said. "How did you sleep?"

"Good." She didn't look up; she was reading the paper.

I said, "Where's Mum?"

"She's gone to work already—a client needed her house done first thing." She folded the paper and said, "So, little sister, wanna do something today."

"Sure? What?"

"I want to see this exhibition at the National Gallery."

"Where's that?"

"Just next to the National Portrait Gallery," she said.

I must have looked blank, because she rolled her eyes. "Trafalgar Square. We'll get the train."

I nodded. "What's the exhibition?"

She passed me a brochure with the details and got up. She went to the counter. "Coffee?" she said.

"Since when do you drink coffee?"

"Since always."

"I'll have tea." I glanced at the brochure and then turned over the paper to the news. Emily sat back down with her coffee.

She said, "I was reading that."

"Where's my tea?" I said.

She put her hand to her mouth in mock surprise. "Sorry," she said sarcastically.

"And to think I was looking forward to you coming home."

"Don't be like that, Soph. I'm sorry. I just couldn't be bothered to make tea. You can have a coffee, though; it's ready." She passed me her cup.

"No, thanks," I replied, and pushed the cup back across the table.

I got up and made myself tea and some toast with peanut butter. Emily told me about her boyfriend. Turned out I hadn't met him. The room was warm. The kitchen table was bright from the sun pouring through the window. The light made everything look angelic. I told Emily this. She laughed. Told me my imagination was on overdrive and I should get out of the house more. She jumped up. "Come on," she said. "We should go."

"It's still really early."

"Teenagers," she said.

"You're still a teenager."

"Only just. Hurry up."

I didn't answer; instead I read the back cover of a book I'd borrowed from the library. It was about three generations of women in the same family, all adventure and tragedy—the sort of book I liked to read during the summer holiday.

Fluffy came in and prowled around the food bowl, and Emily got up to feed her. The cat danced around the bowl in anticipation. Emily's phone rang and she went to talk to whoever it was. She gestured at me and at her watch. I fed Fluffy, who crunched away with pleasure. I wondered if Em was speaking to her boyfriend. I put the dishes in the dishwasher and wiped the counter free of crumbs. Emily always left a mess: clothes lying around, paintings and bits of fabric all over the house.

I took a shower and put on jeans and one of her tops. She gave me a look when she saw me wearing her top but didn't say anything. She was wearing a great skirt and loose layers of jumpers and shirts. If I wore an outfit like that, I'd look like I was trying to be cool, but she made it look arty and good. She had paint on her cheek. She said, "Are you *finally* ready?"

We walked to the station together. She smoked a

cigarette. Something else she'd taken up at art college. She talked about another project, something to do with lost gloves, which made me think of Mum's collection, but I didn't say anything, I just listened and nodded and admired her pretty blond hair as we waited on the platform together. We arrived at King's Cross and changed for the Piccadilly line. It was close and busy on the Underground. We ran to catch a train. Emily got on, but the lace of my trainer was undone and I stumbled. She jumped off to help me, and the doors shut before we had a chance to get back on together. The next train was two minutes away. I didn't think it mattered.

The worst thing Emily ever did was wait for me to tie up my shoelace. If she hadn't waited for me, we'd have been on a different train. If she had made me get on the first train and told me to leave my lace, then everything would be different. And if Mark hadn't gone to play squash, he'd maybe be enjoying his day with Katherine today not knowing his heart was a time bomb.

Everything's a time bomb.

FRIDAY, APRIL 21ST

The temperature has dropped, although it should be getting warmer. I'm sitting outside King's Cross Station wondering what to do with myself. I wish now I'd brought another jumper and some gloves.

I left the house really early today, before Mum got up. I was going to Bowood Road. It was like a mantra. *18 Bowood Road. 18 Bowood Road. 18 Bowood Road.* Not that I know where it is, really. Elephant & Castle somewhere. I figured I'd just go and work it out. So I walked all the way to King's Cross, but then I got stuck outside. Since I got there, hundreds of people passed by, but no one seemed to see me. The air was acrid. People rushed past, looking down.

I watched a man wearing a suit. I imagined blood on his cheek like a jagged, red pen mark. He dove into the entry point of the Underground. I wondered who he was and where he was going, which train he was catching. I wondered if he realized how it was just chance that he wasn't sitting on that train. He'd already forgotten, probably forgot about it the very next day, moved on to his life, his office, his wife or girlfriend. I hated the man suddenly. But then he was gone into the crowd and he didn't matter. Nobody mattered.

I looked at the crush of people passing. I wanted to open out my arms and scream at them that they shouldn't go down there. They shouldn't go into the Underground!

I couldn't go into the train station. I couldn't go in and catch a train. Just the thought of it made me want to weep. In the end I bought a *London A–Z* map book so I could find Bowood Road. If I caught a bus, there was a route I could walk afterward that went past St. Thomas's Hospital, which was where I was born, so I decided to go that way. I caught the bus and then walked REALLY FAR. I had no real idea that London was *so* big. Or so lonely. I mean, I knew in my head it was big, but I've never *felt* it before.

I arrived at St. Thomas's Hospital and looked at the grey boxy windows, trying to picture myself as a baby. Had Emily been brought to visit me? She must have been. I tried to bring the building to life with any memory I had, but I didn't have any. In my imagination the hospital had assumed more importance. Standing there, I realized how many thousands of babies must have been born behind those windows, were probably being born right now. I was no different. Not special, not anything.

I walked south. The streets were filled with little shops and pubs, people busy with their own lives, buses streaming past, cars beeping, the noise and chaos of London.

And I walked and walked.

And then I got there.

Bowood Road is narrow, full of identical terraced houses. I'd hoped to remember something, anything, but if it hadn't been for the photograph, I would never have known our old house. The sun was out, full and warm. I sat on a low wall opposite 18 Bowood Road. At about four in the afternoon a boy came up to number 20 and went in. Ten minutes later he bounded back out like a puppy, smiled quickly at me, and rushed off. He looked about my age, a blond boy with a sweet smile. I smiled back. This blond boy could have been my friend if Dad hadn't died and we hadn't moved away from Bowood Road. We'd have gone to each other's houses all the time and hung out. As babies I bet we played together.

I walked away. My hands were shaking.

I walked on automatic pilot. Ages later I realized I was hungry. I went into one place thinking I might find something to eat, but when I saw everyone was drinking and playing darts or pool, I backed out onto the pavement.

I saw the word *Emily's* on a scruffy building next door, the letters made from red tubular lights. Her name. A restaurant. Inside it was gloomy and empty. It smelled of cooked burgers and the grease of years of frying chips. An old pop song played quietly in the background. A woman with thick yellow-stained glasses stood by the door, cleaning one of the tables. She was thin and beaky, like a half-starved heron. Her movements were really quick.

She said, hardly stopping, "What can I help you with?" and I wondered from her accent if she was Scottish.

"I need something to eat."

"Okay." She gave me a look then and we both paused. I felt like she was weighing me up; I could almost see the darkening of her pupils as she considered something. She said softly, "Are you okay?"

"Just hungry."

"I know the feeling," she said. She leaned over and gave

me a gentle pat on the shoulder. She led me to a table near the back.

I looked at the menu. "I'll have the chicken and chips, please."

"Ketchup?"

I nodded. "And a Coke."

Time floated past. I looked at the photographs of celebrities on the wall. The chicken arrived. I ate everything on the heaped plate. I went up to the counter surrounded by fairy lights, and paid my bill with a torn note.

She said, "Hope you're feeling better. I'm Emily. This is my restaurant. Come back anytime."

I wanted to tell her that her name was my sister's name, that her restaurant was named after my sister. I wanted to tell her I was too frightened to get on the train home, but she was a stranger and so I remained silent.

I left. The evening had slipped by. I phoned Mum and lied and told her that Rosa-Leigh and I were still hanging out. She sighed and said, "I have dinner ready."

"Sorry," I said quickly before I switched off my phone and started walking.

It was a long, lonely walk, and in the end I had to catch two different buses because I was so tired. By the time I got in, it was late. Mum had made a chicken casserole. She'd put my plate in the fridge and gone to bed. I didn't eat it. I wasn't hungry.

SATURDAY, APRIL 22ND

This afternoon, from my spot sunning myself on the roof of our house, I saw Mum coming up the road. She was smiling and talking into her mobile. In her other hand was a bag of shopping. She didn't notice me watching her. Tears trickled from my eyes. I'm going crazy with sadness. I wish I'd never got on the stupid train. I wish I'd tied my shoelaces properly. I lay back and stared at the big empty sky, hoping for answers.

SUNDAY, APRIL 23RD

I woke from a dream where I kissed Dan. I tried to remember him kissing me, and my insides skipped with the memory of his lips, of his hands pressing against me. To make me forget about him, because he hasn't called, I concentrated on the posters of blue and white buildings in Greece on my walls. I looked at the scrawled quotations from my favorite books on my chalkboard. I gazed out the window framed by blue silky curtains looking over a telephone pole populated occasionally with birds.

I can't connect the girl in this room with the girl who was kissing Dan at that party. Nothing feels the same anymore, not even me. I don't know who I am or how I fit into a world I don't understand.

I feel like going to Bowood Road again to look at our

old house. Things in my life were good there. Maybe I'll go now just to pass the endless time.

Everything was horrible. Awful. I don't even understand what happened. I'm so embarrassed. The walk started okay. It was sunny outside when I left the house. I caught a bus and got off near Westminster. It was surprisingly warm. I sweated as I walked, and my throat started to hurt, taking in the dirty, warm air. Central London is so busy and polluted.

The buildings in Westminster are beautiful. I didn't think I cared about buildings, but the Houses of Parliament are so perfect, so stunning, that I can't believe I've never really looked at them before. We've driven past, but I've never stood in front of them like I did today. If I could draw, I'd sketch them. When I try to write about the color of the stone or the shape of the spires and the feeling there of age and history, I can't get the words onto the page. I wish I could. This morning Big Ben rose out of the mist, and despite all the cars and the traffic and the noise, I swear I could feel the past weighing on me. In a good way.

Outside the Houses of Parliament there was a small protest against the war in Iraq. The war seems pointless. Even thinking about it confuses me. Some say the war is making things better. Who for? Not for me. All these people being killed and for what? For religion? It doesn't seem possible. People are angry, people are confused, people are frightened, maybe, but not because of religion.

Dan's family is Muslim, I think, although I'm just guessing, and Kalila's a Muslim, for sure. Megan's a Christian although she's totally unchristian all the time! I'm not anything, I don't think, although Mum occasionally goes to church and I have been a few times. I don't think I even believe in God sometimes. Rosa-Leigh said she is going to become some sort of Buddhist one day. In the end we're all just people.

Just as I arrived at 18 Bowood Road, a girl who looked at least a couple of years older than me took out a bag of rubbish. She put it in the bin and went back inside. Emily *never* took out the rubbish. Never. I wanted to follow the girl inside. I wanted to see where I grew up, where I lived when my family was whole.

So, stupidly, I opened the gate.

The sun made striped patterns on the path. I knocked on the front door. As if she'd been waiting on the other side, the girl who'd taken out the rubbish opened it. She frowned. Her face was closed.

She said, "What?"

"I—" I suddenly had nothing to say. "I'd like to—"

The girl turned before I finished the sentence and called, "Mum," over her shoulder. She faced me again.

151

Except she wasn't looking at me. She was waiting, like a person at a station might wait for a train, not really focusing on anything. I didn't matter to her, because I was a stranger. And so to get her attention, I said, "I used to live here."

Her gaze snapped back to mine, her eyes dark as Emily's. "Oh," she said sarcastically.

I began to feel really stupid. What did it matter where I used to live? What did any of it matter? None of it was going to bring Emily back. I felt a panic attack surging like a tsunami.

I reached out a hand to steady myself. I was finding it hard to breathe. I didn't want to panic in front of this stranger, but thinking that made me feel worse. I said, "I'm sorry to bother you. I just—"

She shook her head as if a fly were buzzing around her.

A woman appeared in the corridor, an older woman, thin face, long, dyed red hair.

The girl at the door said very loudly, "She used to live here, Mum."

I whispered, "I don't know what's wrong with me."

The woman said, "Are you okay?"

I shook my head. And then it was as if the ground rushed up to meet me. "I'm sorry," I said. "Oh God." Nausea rose in my throat. I laid my hand across my mouth to stop myself being sick. "I don't know why I'm here." I looked at them, somehow lost my footing, stumbled, and fell. Hard.

152

The woman pushed past the girl at the door and leaned over me. "Give me some help, Sally," she said to her daughter. The woman got me to a seated position and made me copy her breathing. "That's right, breathe slowly." She squinted at me. "I'm Eleanor Summerfield," she said.

I nodded, struggling not to faint again.

Eleanor said, "Why don't you come in and we'll sort this out?"

The girl, Sally, was back in the house, and she was looking worried. As I followed Eleanor through the short corridor to the kitchen, I looked at the pictures of Sally all along the walls. She was a dancer, it seemed. I tried to remember the house when I'd been in it as a little girl. I had a flash of memory of Emily laughing, trotting along in Mum's high heels.

The kitchen was small and dark, with only a little window. I could picture Mum reading the paper in there. I thought I remembered my dad, the faint shape of him, and then the memory was gone. The kitchen was different from how I thought it would be. Changed.

It smelled of fresh coffee. Eleanor guided me to sit at the plastic table; my hands shook. I said, "I'm sorry." I was going to say something else, but I didn't know what to say, so I sat there with my palms down and tried to steady my breathing. I said, "I don't recognize the house; well, I kind of do. I think we had a round table and maybe there was some sort of plant over there."

"It must have been years since you lived here. We've been here forever." Eleanor switched the kettle on. "We finished the coffee. Make some tea, Sally." She sat next to me.

"I thought I'd remember more. It's just shadows of memory. Shapes. Nothing I can be sure of."

Sally said, "Is she all right?"

"Make it sugary. Should help. There are some clean cups in the dishwasher."

"What's wrong with her?"

"Not sure."

"I think," I said, "I think I'm going mad." I saw a blast of orange light in my mind's eye. Felt the glass of the kitchen window shatter to smithereens in my imagination. I passed one of my hands over my eyes to clear the thoughts.

Eleanor was quiet. The skin around her eyes was very lined. She coughed and her lungs rattled. When I didn't say anything, she said, "Has something happened?" She was very gentle.

I took a deep breath, the panic starting to fade. "I used to live here with my mum, dad, and sister."

Eleanor glanced over at her daughter then back at me. My heart dropped low into my body; how could I explain myself? I said, "There was an accident. No, not an accident."

Sally put three cups and a full teapot down on the table and sat across from me. She smiled, and I saw in her overly

154

big smile, her wide polite eyes, that she thought I wasn't right in the head.

I said, "I just wanted to come here. I know it doesn't make sense." I picked up my cup. "I'm sorry," I said.

Eleanor nodded. "Are you feeling okay?" she asked. Her voice was loud and she spoke slowly, like she was trying to get through on a bad phone line. She reached a hand out and touched me briefly on the arm. "Is there someone we can call?" She poured the tea and stirred two sugars in mine, passing me the cup.

I sipped and tasted the sugary sweetness of the tea. I tried to put everything in place in my head.

Sally said quietly, "I have to go to Dad's, Mum."

"Get Juliette to give you a lift," Eleanor replied. Then more quietly, as if I might not hear her, "This girl needs a moment."

I said, "No, I'm sorry. I should go. I'm in your way." I couldn't stop apologizing.

Eleanor lifted her palm in a *wait-there* gesture. I didn't move.

Sally said, "See you later," and was gone.

I said, "I should go. I've disturbed you enough." My nearly full cup stared at me accusingly.

"Let me know who to call," Eleanor said.

"There's no one to call. It never gets better."

"What about your mum? Or your sister?"

I shook my head. The panic had leached out of me, and

155

I was left feeling empty and ashamed. "I have to go." I was entirely, vividly aware of how humiliating the situation was. This woman was a total stranger.

My head hurt. I rubbed my eyes. "I'm really sorry. I don't know anything anymore."

I stood up and pulled my coat around me. "I should go."

"Let me help you."

I felt as if a flat blade had gone under my rib cage and lifted the bones. I hurried to the corridor, not answering when Eleanor followed, saying, "Are you sure you'll be all right?"

Just as I opened the door, she said, "Come and sit back down. We'll call someone."

I lied, "No, my friend lives nearby. She'll take me home."

And that was it. The door of 18 Bowood Road closed, and I went back out into the road as if nothing had happened. It took me hours to get home.

MONDAY, APRIL 24TH

The Easter holiday is over. I called the reception at school and told them I had the flu. The receptionist went quiet for a moment and then said, "Sophie Baxter. You missed a couple of days at the end of last term and you're ill again?"

"Yeah. I'm just sick."

"You'll need a doctor's note."

I went quiet.

She said, "Baxter. Aren't you the one who was in the—"

I hung up.

10

And, and, and . . .

TUESDAY, APRIL 25TH

I climbed onto the roof and sat there staring into space. I kept thinking I could see Emily. Or hear her voice. But not what she was saying.

I think I'm dying. I can't breathe. And I don't want to remember the day of the bombing, but I can't stop myself. I remember standing on the platform with Emily. I remember exactly what I said and every word she spoke back to me in reply.

I remember I finished tying my shoelace and said, "Sorry, Em."

"Not to worry. There'll be another train in a minute."

"What are we going to see again?"

"A show at the National Gallery. Light boxes. Sound good?"

"And after that?"

"I don't know, what do you feel like?" she said.

It was hot. Very crowded. I looked at the other passengers on the platform. One tall guy farther down caught my eye. He smiled. The train roared in. We got on.

Emily held the crook of my arm as we squeezed into seats, thinking ourselves lucky to sit on such a packed train, and then she let go. Between the gaps in the people, in the black glass opposite, I looked at myself and Emily. We looked so different, Emily and I. Me, dark-haired and pale; her, blond-haired, dark-eyed.

The train pulled out of the station, swaying so we pressed against each other, arm to arm in our seats. The tunnel was black around us.

Emily started to say something.

There was a flash of orange light, a huge bang.

I saw her face for a split second, her eyes wide and her mouth falling open in a scream.

Then the explosion burst the reflection of Emily and me to smithereens. Glass sprayed in silver lines and I flung my hands to my eyes. A force pushed into the back of me and my whole spine jolted, my chest jarred up into my throat. I was twisted and thrown in a vat of scalding air. Every part of my body was slammed and shocked, and I thought I saw a huge fireball blast toward me, but it may have been the searing of the insides of my eyes. I smashed down and lay momentarily very still. The air stank of burned hair, and much worse.

Someone was screaming; it could have been me. From the feel against my palms I thought I could tell that I was pressed against the ridged floor of the train, but I couldn't see anything in the dark. I tried to stand, but something was crushing me. I fought in the blackness and shoved a heavy object off my leg.

I managed to get to my feet, and then I coughed and was nearly sick. The object I'd thrown off me, it seemed, was my seat. There was smoke and glass everywhere. Someone yelled, "Help me, please! Help me!" I touched my fingers to my face and felt wet, warm and wet. Was it blood? Tears?

My head was ringing. "Emily," I croaked, frantic and dizzy. Everything was screaming. My ears were violent suddenly, assaulting me with the sounds of other voices. I put my hands before me. A light flickered on and off. And on. I saw Emily. I screamed and I knew it was me screaming because my throat tore as the sound came out.

She was lying not far from me in the wreckage of the train interior. Her neck was in the wrong position. Her limbs were all at strange angles. I fought my way over to her, screaming her name. The layers of her shirts were half

160

torn off. I could see the dirty, pale skin of her shoulder. Her eyes were semi-closed.

"Emily," I sobbed. "You'll be okay. You'll be okay. Stay with me."

The air stank of sweat, of fire, of fear. My words evaporated into the chaos and dust around us.

"Emily, listen to me. Hold on. I'll get help."

She squeezed my hand. My ears roared. She was struggling to breathe.

"Sophie," she whispered.

"Don't speak, don't speak. Save your breath until someone comes." I begged the air for help. All I could see were smoke and the shadow of a crush of people looming and fading. I feared we'd be trampled. I turned back to Emily. She was trying to get air in, making these small gasping movements with her mouth like a fish out of water.

She managed to whisper, "It hurts."

She took a ragged breath.

And then her eyes rolled.

And then everything stopped.

I yelled her name. I tried to help her breathe by blowing air into her mouth. I tried to get her heart to work again by pounding at her chest. I shook her and I held her and I screamed.

The tall guy was beside me. Blood welled from his cheek, the cut a jagged red pen line. He said, "We need to get out."

He looked down at me, and his eyes were so kind I wept.

"I've got to stay with her," I said, tears falling all over my cheeks and dripping salty into my mouth.

He made the tiniest no motion with his head and kept his gaze locked on mine. He repeated, "We need to get out. You need to follow me." He grabbed my wrist, a manacle, and pulled me with him.

We half crawled out of the train. One woman had so much glass in her hair, she looked like a dusty snow queen. I put my hand up to my own hair and found it to be full of glass, too. I saw a man lying on the tracks. I couldn't work out if he was moving. The tall man held my wrist, following a man wearing an orange jacket. We were caught up in a strange, silent flow of people. I yelled to the man in orange, "My sister. She's back there. I need help. I left her."

A voice came over the loudspeaker. "Don't panic. Stay calm." Then the voice tore up and crackled out of existence.

One man took photos with his phone. Another ran past yelling that he was going to die. Someone near the front seized him and yelled, "Calm down. You've got to calm down."

I kept walking. The tall man had his fingers tight around my wrist. We stumbled along the tunnel and then up a flight of stairs. Twice I struggled and tried to go back but was forced up and up.

We stepped out into the light. I blinked. Paramedics

rushed around. Flashing blue lights illuminated dozens of people with blood on their faces. There was blood on the grey tarmac beneath my feet, and the sky above was cloudy, buildings filling the space between. Next to me stood a woman with black ash like runny mascara on her cheeks. I rubbed my face and the same blackness came off on my fingers.

I took a deep breath and looked at the people everywhere. I stumbled one way, stopped and turned to go back down.

A police officer said, "You can't go in there."

"Emily," I whispered. I staggered away from him. A woman put her arm around my shoulders to direct me. I let her lead, and she helped me into an ambulance. A journalist pushed a microphone into my face, and I turned away.

I must have fainted because, when I woke, I was lying in a bed in a brightly lit room. I struggled to focus.

"What's happened?" came a voice, and it took me a moment to see my mother leaning over me, fluorescent light in her hair and eyes. She said, out of breath, "Oh my God. Look at you. Are you okay? I just got here. I can't believe I found you." She wrapped me in a hug. She smelled of her perfume, her shampoo.

I pushed her off, saying, "Where am I?" I fought to sit. "What's going on?"

"Are you okay? It took me ages to get here. I've been desperate. How are you feeling? Where's Emily?" Mum's eyes were wet. "She's with you?"

I shook my head.

Mum said, "They directed me here to find—" She looked around. "Where is she? Where is she?"

"She was with me. She was right next to me."

Mum said, "Where is she, Sophie?"

"What's happened?" I said.

A doctor appeared and put his hand on my upper arm. He said, "There was a bomb. They've blown up a train. What's your name? You're badly bruised, but nothing's broken. You're in shock."

I tried to speak.

Mum squeezed my fingers. The doctor smiled gently at her, and she released me from her grip. She was crying. She said, "Her name's Sophie Marie Baxter. I'm her mother. Her older sister was with her. Emily Baxter. She must be here somewhere. Oh my God."

The doctor called out, "Have we got an Emily Baxter here?"

I said, "She was with me on the train. She's my sister."

A nurse appeared around the door, looked at a clipboard, and shook her head. Then she looked at us and said, "It's total pandemonium. There's been another explosion out there—several, they think. A terrorist attack. Suicide bombers, perhaps—they don't know. Wait here."

"I need to find my daughter. My other daughter is missing. Why won't anyone tell me what's going on?" Mum had tears running down both cheeks and her arms folded over her chest. She dashed the tears away and folded her arms again. "Please find my daughter."

"I was in the train," I said. The words I needed to say would not come out.

"She's in shock," said the doctor, not to me. "Cuts and bruises, some temporary damage to her hearing. It's not as bad as it looks. She's very lucky."

A couple appeared at the doorway, and I thought they were familiar. They stared at me hopefully then looked at each other in dismay. I clearly wasn't who they were looking for—they were strangers after all.

Mum said my sister's name, walked away, came back. She was like a headless chicken flailing for life when life was gone.

"Mum, Emily's still down there," I finally said. And again I fainted.

THURSDAY, APRIL 27TH

Before I left the house for school, Mum tried to talk to me. I said, "I have to run. I'm late."

"Sophie, could we have supper together?"

I paused and looked back at her. Under her eyes she had dark purple rings that might be there permanently now.

She smiled. I surprised myself by saying, "Why do you collect lost things?"

Her eyebrows furrowed. She said, "They're not lost things in my collection. They're things I've found."

Her answer made no sense. I said, "I'm late for school," and headed out the door.

I heard her call after me, "What about supper?"

FRIDAY, APRIL 28TH

On my way home from school today I was walking slowly, dreading getting there. I was looking at the ground, and I didn't notice someone approaching me. Ended up, I slammed headfirst into Dan! I blushed and my stomach lurched.

"Sophie," he said, dipping his head so he could look into my eyes, which made me blush more.

I knew I looked a mess, and I was wearing my school uniform, which was completely embarrassing. I pushed my hands through my hair.

He said, "I've been meaning to call you."

"To say what?"

"That I want to see you again."

"It's been ages. Too long," I said.

"Doesn't mean I haven't been thinking about you."

My heart jumped. "What about Abigail? She's your girlfriend."

166

He shook his head. "It just sort of happened that way." He put a hand on my cheek, and my skin burned. "I loved kissing you. You felt so good. You're so pretty. It's you I like."

Despite the fact I haven't heard from him, despite the fact that he and Abi are still together, I couldn't help but tip my face up. He leaned closer and brushed his lips against mine. My stomach did a slow flip and my insides gathered tightly.

"Oh, Dan," I sighed, which sounds really stupid, but it made him groan and kiss me harder. Suddenly I didn't care about Abigail, or Mum, or Emily, or anything, and all I could think about was how good I felt.

He pulled away and said, "Do you want to come back to my house? We could have a drink, spend some time together?"

I felt my cheeks warm, and I smiled. "Sure." I nodded.

Just then his mobile rang. He lightly touched my cheek and said, "Let me get this." He pulled the phone out of his pocket and turned away. He said, "Hey, you," before he stepped out of my hearing. I bet it was Abigail. I cringed with frustration at myself.

I looked at him, my heart still beating fast and my mouth still tasting of him. Despite it all, I was going to go back to his house. I shivered in anticipation. It would be so good to forget everything, to spend a few hours in his arms. He winked over at me and then got off the phone.

I said, "Okay, let's go."

"I'm sorry, Sophie, honey. That was a friend of mine. I have to go—I already have plans. Kissing you made me forget."

I barely had time to stammer a good-bye before he gave me a quick kiss on the lips and hurried off up the road. He yelled over his shoulder, "I'll call you." Then he was gone, almost as if nothing had just happened between us. I had a pain go through me at the thought that he was on his way to see Abigail, but it didn't stop me liking him. I put my fingers to my lips. I knew deep down that kissing Dan was never going to make anything better. I knew Emily would have told me the same thing. But I pushed the thought aside.

TUESDAY, MAY 2ND

In the lunch queue I heard Abigail say to Megan, "Dan still hasn't called. He promised he'd come and see me on Friday. I texted him asking where he was, but he said he was busy doing something with his mum. I didn't hear from him all weekend. I want to see him."

Megan glanced back at Zara and gave her a secret smile with her big toothy mouth. I couldn't interpret it at all. I hate Megan. Worse, I hate myself for kissing Dan and for being pleased he didn't see Abi on Friday. I was delighted he hadn't left me to go and see her. He'd gone to see his mum!

Although, I thought he said he was going to see a friend. I thought of him bending forward to kiss me, of how he made that groan when I said his name. I like him so much. When did everything get so complicated?

I was glad when Abi bought a huge plate of chips with a burger. She's so thin her bones almost push at her skin. She's lost a lot of weight recently.

I sat down with Megan and Abi, hoping Rosa-Leigh would show up soon. The girls queuing for their food shoved and jostled each other. Everything was so normal. Except for me. The blood in my veins pulsed a sudden, strange, silent flow of terror. My heart starting thumping. A panic attack. I left my food and, without telling the others where I was going, hurried to the bathroom, where I hid in one of the stalls hoping to calm down.

I heard people come in. The first one said, "How quick can you do it?" It was Megan, I could recognize her nasal voice anywhere.

"Maybe ten seconds." The other was Abigail.

"Okay, you take the toilet on the right. I'll race you."

I had no idea what they were talking about. Then I heard them go into the stalls, and they both started retching. THROWING UP. It was revolting.

I stayed really quiet.

After a while they stopped and came out of the stalls. The bathroom stank of sick.

Abigail said, "I feel better. I can't believe I ate all that."

169

Megan said, "I had so many chips. All gone now." There was a pause. She said, "You look great. You know Zara can do it in five seconds."

There was the sound of taps running, and then the water was turned off.

Then they walked out of the bathroom together, their voices cut off as the door clicked shut behind them.

WEDNESDAY, MAY 3RD

How could I not have noticed what's been going on with Abi?

FRIDAY, MAY 5TH

All I've thought about all week is Abi. I didn't even realize my best friend was making herself so sick. How could I be so blind? God, everything's so messed up. I'm so messed up.

I think I'm permanently panicking. Abi and I hardly speak right now, so I can't ask her about her problems. Not that I'd know where to start. But I feel sorry for her. Then I feel sorry for me. I don't know what to do.

MONDAY, MAY 8TH

I had to see Lynda today. I sat down and felt the usual tension. She said, "I could refer you to another therapist if you think you might like it. She's very good. I wonder if you might want to talk to her."

I said, "You're quitting on me?"

"No, you can keep coming to see me if you want. You're always welcome here. I'm just not sure I've been able to give you the help I think you need."

I went quiet and thought about what she was saying. I thought about how messed up I am.

She said, "Let's take it one step at a time. It's up to you. What do you think would be best?" She smiled her pleading puppy-dog smile. The one that makes me so cross with her. I realized suddenly it wasn't her fault.

I said, "I'm sorry I haven't been able to talk to you. I don't know why."

"It's okay. What would you like to do?"

"I'd like to see the other therapist. It's nothing personal. I think I need to start over. With someone else."

She nodded.

I said, "The writing has been helpful, though. Thank you for giving me the notebook."

She smiled, and there was nothing else to say.

WEDNESDAY, MAY 10TH

I have so much homework, I haven't had time to write anything. Abi still looks awful. Dan hasn't called. I'm avoiding Mum. And I've got so much homework to do and exams to study for. I'm having trouble sleeping. Not that I wasn't already.

SATURDAY, MAY 13TH

I woke in the early morning because it's Emily's birthday today. She'd be twenty. I lay in the dark thinking about her. I tried to picture what she'd look like now, but I couldn't. In my imagination she looked just the same as the last morning I saw her.

I wonder if one day she'd have been a great artist. Or teacher. Or social worker. I can imagine her in a job where she helped other people. I wonder if in the future she'd have married and had kids.

A slow anger burned through me. She'd never have children now. I'll never be an aunt. God, I want to see my sister on her birthday.

SUNDAY, MAY 14TH

I worked on that poem again. I thought of a last verse.

The sticks on the trees
Stand up harsh and bare
With rings on their fingers
And knots in their hair

The silver of winter
Is smoky with rain
The witches of sunlight
Fly low again

In a puddle of grey
Last summer lies
Where nothing can swim
And my sister dies

In front of my eyes

WEDNESDAY, MAY 17TH

God, I wish I could go back to the night I was sitting with Emily on the roof. I wish I could hold time still at that moment and never move forward. I wish I could be there forever.

THURSDAY, MAY 18TH

I got home from school, and I pushed my bedroom door shut behind me. I hadn't time to catch my breath before I was on my knees crying. And then I saw Emily. I could see her lying there on the floor in front of me, struggling for breath. Why did this happen? What sort of a world is it where someone could do something like this? Why my sister? What did she ever do to anyone? Why did she die and not me?

Then, instead of lying there in the tunnel, Emily was standing in front of me wearing jeans and a gold dress cut off at the thighs.

"That's my dress," I said.

She shook her head.

"You can have it," I said.

And I knew she wasn't there. I know she's not here. But for a moment I felt better. My sister.

11

The spring is weighted
With what has been

FRIDAY, MAY 19TH

I had to get out of the house this evening, so I called Rosa-Leigh and we arranged that I'd go over. Her dad said he'd give us a ride to Camden so we could go to the spoken-word thing—I don't think he realizes it's in a bar.

"Where've you been?" she said when I eventually arrived.

"The bus took forever."

"I don't mean that.

"What do you mean?"

"You've been walking around school in a fog for ages. Since Easter."

"I was just—" I paused. "I was just thinking."

Her dad drove us there, making jokes on the way. Rosa-Leigh looked at me a couple of times, and as soon as we got out of the car, she grabbed me and said, "What's going on? You're not telling me something."

There was so much I wasn't telling everyone. I blurted out the first thing that came to mind. "I kissed Dan."

"Oh my God," she said. "And are you okay?" She was talking fast and pushing me into the room, and I sat on one of the sofas and took a deep breath.

She brought me a drink and said, "Why didn't you tell me?" Her face was open, surprised. "He's the worst, Sophie."

"What do you mean?"

"Sorry to tell you this, but Kalila heard from Zara that he and Megan are, you know, sleeping together."

"Dan slept with *Megan*?" I put my hand over my mouth, and my stomach twisted with jealousy. "No." But suddenly it made sense. He'd had no qualms about kissing Abi's old best friend, me, so why would he have any trouble sleeping with her new one, Megan? I wondered if it was Megan who'd called when he'd been kissing me in the street. And then I thought of the look Megan had given Zara in the lunch queue. It *was* her! He'd gone to see *her* that night when he'd left me. It was true. God, I'd been so wrapped up in everything else, I hadn't realized what sort of a guy he really is.

"What?" Rosa-Leigh said. "You didn't like him?"

I said, "I did. I really liked him. I'm an idiot."

"*He's* an idiot. God, that's why you've been hiding away? Because of some guy?"

"Does Abigail know about Megan?"

"I don't think she does." She took a big sip of her drink. "Tell me everything."

"I don't even know where to start."

"When was it?"

I leaned back into the sofa and took a deep breath. "It was stupid. It was nothing."

There was a silence, and then Rosa-Leigh said, "It was at her party, right?"

"Kind of. Yes."

"I knew it."

"And then I ran into him on my way home from school. Oh God. I kissed him again."

"No!"

I smiled at her. "Dumb. Really dumb." I thought of Dan kissing me. I thought of how his hands touched me. I said, "Is Abigail okay?"

"I don't know."

"Abigail has a lot to deal with right now without having to worry about him. And what you asked before: is it because of him I've been spaced out. The answer's no. It's not him. It's me thinking about what happened to me last summer. I've been thinking about my sister a lot."

Rosa-Leigh nodded. "Do you want to talk about it?"

I shook my head. "Not yet. That's what was nice about Dan. It was easy to forget."

Rosa-Leigh gave me a brief nod and kindly changed the subject. "Kalila's coming to meet us here. She's the coolest person." Rosa-Leigh smiled. "Except for maybe you."

And then Kalila arrived. She was wearing her head scarf, as usual, and she looked good. It's funny: I've never really talked to her, and since last summer, I feel really uncomfortable. I don't blame her—that would be stupid. I blame the people who did it, those hateful men. But I worry she might think I'm blaming her because she's a Muslim—even though that's ridiculous. I know other people have given her a hard time, especially last term, especially stupid Megan. But I've just avoided her.

She sat and said, "Hi."

I had that feeling again, the one I always get when I'm with her, like I don't know what to say. I don't want her to feel uncomfortable, either. I said, "Hi" back and then didn't have any other words. I was thinking about the tunnel, about the shattering of glass, and my mouth went dry. I started to feel sick.

She said, "Are you okay?"

I shrugged and took a couple of deep breaths. "I don't

know. No, yes, I'm fine," I replied. "I'm sorry, Kalila. I just get, um . . ." I looked to Rosa-Leigh for help.

Rosa-Leigh said, "She just gets freaked out sometimes."

Kalila nodded. And then she just tackled it straight on. She came out and said, "It must have been hard for you. My mum's coworker was there that day."

"Really?" I said. "Is she okay?"

Kalila shrugged. "Kind of. She nearly wasn't. The whole thing makes me sick," she said. "So violent, so stupid, so terrible. It must have been so terrible." She put a hand out and gently touched mine. "It doesn't compare, but it's been horrible for us." She lifted both hands toward herself. "One guy came up to me in the street and spat at me. He called me a terrorist."

"God, that's awful," I said, looking into her gentle dark eyes.

"I understand people being angry, but they should be angry with the right people—with the terrorists, not people like me. I just wish they wouldn't be so narrow-minded."

I nodded. "It's so messed up."

Rosa-Leigh said, "I don't mean to get you guys on to more cheerful things— Well, I do, actually. I thought that you"—she looked at me—"might like to read tonight."

"Read where?"

"Up there. I thought you'd like to read one of your poems."

I shook my head. "I don't think so," I said louder than I meant to.

Rosa-Leigh did a dramatic sigh and said, "Worth a try."

Then Kalila asked me about the poems I've written, and I got a bit shy. She told us how she loves to sing. One of the performance poets started.

I had this feeling in my chest like I wished I'd put my name down to read.

I'm at Rosa-Leigh's house. I called Mum and told her I'm spending the night, and Saturday night, too, if she didn't mind. She sighed and said, "Sure."

SUNDAY, MAY 21ST

When I got home, this MAN came out of the kitchen. I practically had a heart attack, and I was about to start screaming about intruders and stuff when Mum called loudly, "What do you want to eat?" And I could tell by the tone of her voice she wasn't talking to me.

He was a slender man, bald, glasses, round face. I recognized him but I didn't know where from. He reached out his hand and he said his name was Robin.

I shook his hand, which totally enveloped mine.

He said, "I'm so glad to see you. We've met before."

"No, we haven't," I said. I dropped his hand quick,

like it was suddenly hot.

"You were tiny at the time. You wouldn't remember."

Mum came out of the kitchen and jumped at the sight of me. Her face put itself back on, and she tried to smile like everything was completely normal. She said, "Robin and I have been friends for years." She looked up at him.

"What's he doing here?" I said.

"This is my friend, Sophie."

I wanted to say, *And he stayed over last night?*

As if she'd read my mind, she said, "He came over for an early lunch."

I didn't reply, instead turning to go upstairs.

"Come back," Mum called after me. "Join us for lunch, please?"

I ignored her and went to my room. I lay on my bed. I sort of expected something to happen but nothing did.

In the end I went downstairs. They both quieted when I sat down with them. I could see Mum was about to say something, but then Robin gave her this *hold-off* look. Mum sighed and put pasta on my plate. They chatted about some professor they'd known at university—they went to university together, apparently. The conversation felt like it was better off without me in it, so I stayed silent and toyed with my spaghetti. I noticed a yellow spill of olive oil on the table. Since when did Mum start cooking again? I suddenly realized she'd been cooking for me for a while—I just hadn't been eating with her.

Then Mum said, "Robin has been looking forward to meeting you," and added randomly, "He's traveled all over the world."

Robin said, "It's true."

"Why don't you ask him about it?" Mum said.

Robin said, "Don't push her."

"She can do what she wants," I said.

"Sophie, please."

"What? What do you expect? You're acting like everything should be FINE."

Mum's face went red and splotchy all along the sides. She held on to the table, her knuckles white.

"I'm not hungry," I said, and got up.

She said, "Please, Sophie."

I looked at Mum. "What do you want me to say?"

"Please," she said in a whisper.

I could feel Robin staring at me. I knew he just wanted me to sit down, and I hated him for that. And I hated myself for being such a bitch, but I couldn't calm down. I didn't know what to say, so I said, "I'm finished with lunch. I'm going to my room."

Mum yelled after me to come back and talk. I heard Robin saying, "Leave her. Give her time."

"She hates me," said Mum.

I wanted to kill them both.

* * *

182

I slept all afternoon. When I woke up, Robin was gone. I wished then that he hadn't left, because somehow he got in the way of Mum and me. Without him we're back to where we've always been.

I want to tell Mum that I'm sorry. I want to make it better. But she's so nervous around me now, and angry, that I don't know how to handle it.

WEDNESDAY, MAY 24TH

School: awful. Home: worse. Rosa-Leigh called and asked if I wanted to go over tomorrow just for supper. I'll definitely go. Mum is treating me like I'm made of glass and if she drops me I'll break into little bits. I just want her to come and talk to me and make everything okay. But every time she's tried recently, I've yelled at her and shut her out. Perhaps I've ruined everything forever, especially after how I acted during the weekend.

THURSDAY, MAY 25TH

Supper at Rosa-Leigh's was great. It's so much easier there than here with Mum.

FRIDAY, MAY 26TH

I wonder if Emily hadn't died in the bombing whether

she'd have died soon after anyway. Like in that film I can't remember the name of where they're meant to die in a roller-coaster accident but don't. Afterward, death stalks them all until they're killed in horrible ways.

I imagine a big room with lots of pens writing out the dates we're due to die. Fate. Written in the stars. When our date comes, it's all over.

I wonder if there's anything afterward, like God or Allah. Or is there nothing? Is Emily really nothing now? When I remember her, she's so much more than nothing.

Mum came in just now. She said to me, "I love you, Sophie. Don't ever forget that."

I pretended to be asleep. She turned out the light.

MONDAY, MAY 29TH

Abigail looks really sick. She's so thin. It's so obvious that she's throwing up her food, I can't believe I didn't notice before. I can't believe I haven't done anything since that day I found out. I know I should do something, but I feel like we're on two sides of a huge river, and the river is so big that I can't swim across to her even if I want to. Half-term starts tomorrow for the rest of the week; I'll use the breather from homework and tests to try and think of what I can do to help her.

I went to an appointment with a new therapist, the one Lynda organized for me. She is tall and thin and black and looks nothing like Lynda. Her name is (Professor) Koreen Sinclair. She reached out a hand to shake and said, "Hello. Make yourself comfortable."

She isn't annoying or patronizing, or a puppy dog like Lynda. She's firm and clear. I liked her straightaway.

She said, "So, why don't you start by telling me what's brought you here?"

It's so embarrassing, but I just burst into tears. I cried as if an upsurge of water had burst from a pipe deep inside me. Then, after she'd handed me a tissue, I started talking. And I'd only said a couple of things when I started to feel that terrible pounding of my heart. "Oh God, I'm sorry," I said. Nausea flooded through me, and I was struggling to breathe. "I feel like . . . there's no air . . ."

She looked at me as if I was totally normal. She said, "Do you know what a panic attack is?"

I shook my head. I tried to speak. It took a moment for the words to come out. "I looked on the internet, and I wondered if that's what is happening to me. But it seems like the sort of thing that happens to, I don't know, weak people."

She shook her head. "Take a deep breath. Are you okay?"

For the first time in a long time I was honest. "No, I'm not."

"Panic attacks aren't a sign of weakness. A panic attack is a normal physical response that happens at the wrong time. Do you understand?"

"Not really."

"Think of it as a huge adrenaline rush. If you were having that adrenaline rush at the right time, it wouldn't feel remotely strange." Her voice was so calm it was like warm milk.

"Like when?"

"If a little boy stepped out in front of a car and you had to rescue him, for example. Your heart would speed up, sounds would be louder, colors brighter, your digestive system would go on hold so more energy could be diverted into saving him."

"But I've never had to save anyone from stepping in front of a car."

"And that's why it feels so awful. When you panic, you're having that response—a right response—at the wrong time. We'll talk about this again. It'll take a while."

I nodded. Stayed quiet. Caught my breath. Felt my heartbeat return to normal. She smiled. Asked me to come back next week.

When I came out of her cozy room, I felt a little different. Clearer.

12

And she's still with me

Brightly unseen

SUNDAY, JUNE 4TH

I got home from a walk. Robin and Mum were sitting together looking at photographs. I leaned over. There were pictures of them aged about nineteen, hugging each other, sitting on his motorbike, generally looking happy. I said, "When did you two meet?"

Mum gave Robin a quick look and then smiled at me. "We went out together in school. We traveled to Calcutta on his bike when we were twenty-one."

187

I was so astounded that I didn't know what to say. I didn't even know that Mum has been to India. She showed me pictures of her in these crazy, beautiful places. I wished Robin wasn't there, because I felt kind of close to her for the first time in forever. But he was there, and he started telling stories about having no money and sleeping at the sides of the roads. Then he went into great detail about one day when he was robbed in Nepal. I wanted to scream at them, asking why I'd never even heard of Robin. Instead I listened and looked at the pictures. I blurted out, "Why haven't we met before?"

Mum said, "Robin came back into my life, as a friend, six months before Emily died."

It's the first time I've heard her say it out loud. That Emily has died. It caught me in the stomach, her saying it like that, caught me like someone was pulling me backward.

I was about to reply, but my mobile rang. It was ABIGAIL asking if I wanted to come over on Friday night. Even though we've been so distant recently, I know I have to help her with the whole bulimia thing so I said yes.

I was going to ask how she was, but she was in a hurry. When I got off the phone, Mum looked at her watch and said they had to go; they were meeting friends. There was no time to ask any more questions. She looked at me like she felt guilty or sorry or something, but I sort of smiled back to let her know I didn't mind her going out.

I'm lying here trying to imagine Mum and Robin with their friends at some pub or somewhere, and I realize I can't picture them at all. I can't remember what Robin looks like even though I saw him earlier today.

I don't want to go to school tomorrow. I've got Art first thing. I wish I hadn't chosen it. I'm the worst artist in the world.

THURSDAY, JUNE 8TH

Mum made me go to this Boxercise class with her tonight after school. It's not something she's ever even mentioned before, but she wanted us to try it together. She *thought it would be good for us.*

We got there, and Mum said hi in a trying-to-be-friendly way to a couple of the other women standing around in the badly lit big gym, and I realized she'd been there before. The instructor came in: a huge man called Wayne. He gave us all huge gloves and showed us some moves.

We had to pair up and hit our partner—well, not hit her but hit this red padded thing our partner held. Mum was my partner, and she seemed really focused. She even laughed at one point. It was kind of fun.

Then, in the car on the way home, I suddenly wished Emily were there so badly that my heart hurt. I turned my head and looked out the window as the silent streets slipped by.

I wrote a letter to Eleanor Summerfield at 18 Bowood Road today. I wrote that I'm sorry I bothered her. When I finished the letter, I went to post it, and I felt briefly happy. It's been so long since I was happy that I hardly recognized the feeling—then I felt guilty for being happy. And confused.

I'm just about to go to Abigail's now. Robin's giving me a lift there, which is nice of him, I suppose.

When I got to Abigail's, her brother was home. He dragged me off to the living room before she even knew I'd arrived. He said, "What's wrong with Abigail? She looks awful."

I wasn't going to say anything—I felt really disloyal—so I changed the subject and said, "I didn't know you were home."

"Sophie, she's so thin." He stared right at me.

"She's fine."

"What's wrong with her? You must know."

"We're not really that close anymore," I said.

"Sophie," he begged.

He looked so desperate, I had to tell him. I spoke softly. "I think she's bulimic."

He paused. "When you throw up after eating? That?"

I nodded.

"Why haven't you done something? Or said something?"

190

"I didn't even realize myself until recently. I've been, um, distracted, I guess."

He stepped back, releasing me with his eyes, and said, "Bulimic. Are you sure?"

Then I saw Abigail was standing behind him. A tear slid down her cheek, and I knew she'd overheard. She said, "I don't know what to do," really quietly.

Her brother took two strides over and seized her in this big hug. I looked at the floor. I heard him say, "I'll help you, Abi. Just tell me what to do." He let her go. "I'll let you two talk." With that he left the room.

I HAVE NEVER BEEN SO UNCOMFORTABLE IN MY WHOLE ENTIRE LIFE. Abigail and I stared at each other. I could almost feel the river between us, wet and rushing past.

She said, "I'm so sorry about Emily."

I swallowed.

"I really am sorry. I can't believe what it must have been like being there. I can't even imagine it. And you must be so angry with the bombers, and you've seen such terrible things, and I've been such a bitch to you. It's so fucked up."

"I miss her all the time," I said. "Do you remember how she always bossed me around? I was always saying I hated her."

"Not always."

I swallowed and said, "I wish I wasn't so frightened all the time. And so angry."

191

Abigail repeated, "I can't even imagine." She took a deep breath. "I wish I'd been a better friend to you. I didn't really know how."

"I didn't make it easy for you. I didn't know how to talk to anyone about what happened. It wasn't just you. I'm sorry. Really sorry." And then I stepped forward and hugged her. I decided never to tell her about Dan—I realized that sometimes even best friends don't have to know everything about each other.

She said, "Are you okay?"

I shrugged. "Not really. I want to be okay, but I'm not. Not even close." I paused then said, "I probably won't be okay for a long time. Over Easter I went to where my family first used to live."

"Where's that?"

"Bowood Road. Doesn't matter. I don't even know why I'm telling you."

"What was it like? Did you remember it?"

"I couldn't remember anything. I don't even know why I went. I suppose I wanted to understand better. I wanted to know what it was like before."

She said, "I get what you mean."

"I know what's happening with you because I overheard you talking to Megan in the bathroom. You two were making yourselves sick."

"Oh God. Everything's felt so out of control. I couldn't cope with what had happened to you, and to Emily last

192

summer. And Mum's drinking is out of control, and I didn't know how to handle it, and then suddenly I was losing weight. I felt better, and I looked good, and I had some control, I suppose, over things going on around me."

I took a deep breath.

Abigail said, "I don't know what to do."

"I can help."

"No. I think I need proper help."

I felt like everything was spinning. I said, "So do I. I was going to this therapist called Lynda who drove me insane. I went to another one recently because I'm so crazy. I have panic attacks. All the time." I went to sit on the sofa. "How did we both end up such a mess?"

"Speak for yourself," she said, but she was joking. When she put it like that, it was kind of funny, and I burst out laughing. She sat next to me.

I said, "And we seemed so together last year." And it might not sound funny written down, but she laughed and I laughed and then we were both laughing really hard.

Her brother came in and said, "It's not *funny*," and that made us both laugh harder. He smiled and shook his head. "I'll talk to you both later."

TUESDAY, JUNE 13TH

Too much homework. Rosa-Leigh told me that school finishes for the summer much earlier in Canada. She

193

can't believe how many weeks we have left before the holidays.

FRIDAY, JUNE 16TH

Very dull week at school. Mum said we're going to the Haywoods' tonight to stay over. ROBIN IS COMING WITH US. She's already told me TWICE. I wanted to ask her where Robin is going to sleep; is he going to sleep in her room there? What is going on with them? But I couldn't look her in the eye.

SUNDAY, JUNE 18TH

We could tell we were early because Katherine still had an apron on when she opened the door. "Come in, come in," she said, wiping her hands down her front. Then she gave Robin a BIG HUG. Before me or even Mum. She took both of his hands, smiled, and said, "We're so glad to see you, Rob."

Then Katherine hugged me. Just before she let me go, she whispered into my ear, "He's a good person." Then she stepped back, giving me a *significant* look. Every time I think I'm getting closer to being an adult, one of them goes and does something that makes me feel like a child. Katherine got even more annoying. She made this sound like someone had stepped on her foot, and tears spilled out her eyes. She hugged Mum hard.

I was glad to get to Lucy's room. She was sitting on her bed, all breathy and red-faced. "Kai and I have broken up," she said. "I thought I didn't love him, so I dumped him and kissed his friend." She burst into tears. "He won't take me back now." She looked up at me guiltily. "God, I'm sorry to go on about me like this when you've been through so much."

"It's fine. Have you spoken to him?" I said.

"He won't answer his phone. I haven't even been writing my blog; I feel so miserable." She played with her duvet and went all quiet.

The twins shrieked into the room. "You've got the lurgies," Molly cried.

"Get out! This is MY ROOM!" Lucy screamed.

Mark came in and yelled at everyone. Everyone went quiet, because we were all thinking that he'd had a heart attack and he could have died. Well, that's what I was thinking anyway. Then the twins ran out.

Lucy said, "Sorry, Dad." And then to me, "Should we go and find the others?"

I nodded, and the both of us went into the kitchen, where Mum and Katherine were trying to teach Robin to make a roast dinner.

Mum was obviously happy—not insanely happy, but a bit happier. I know I should be pleased for her, but I just feel weird about the whole thing between her and Robin, even though they didn't sleep in the same room because Mum told Katherine they are just friends, for now . . . I overheard her.

I don't know how I feel about any of it. Am I supposed to like him? I hardly know him. It's been so long since I've seen Mum happy like this that I know I should be nice to him, but then he does something annoying, like putting his hand on Mum's arm, which he MUST know is completely awkward for me. And how does Emily fit into the whole picture? She never met Robin and isn't part of this new family. Are we a new family? Is Mum in love with Robin? Or are they really just friends?

I wish Emily were around to talk to because . . . Just because.

WEDNESDAY, JUNE 21ST

Dan texted just now. Unbelievable. He says he's been thinking about me. He wants to meet. A tiny part of me thought about kissing him, thought about how easy it was, how it made me forget everything else. But the rest of me remembered what a jerk he's been to Abigail. Sleeping with Megan, fooling around with me while seeing Abi. I'm never going to see him again.

I was going to reply, saying something like "Not now, not ever," but I figured answering would only encourage him. I deleted his text. And his number. Exactly what Emily would have done.

Between Art and English Abigail told me she was going to break up with Dan. "He's not really that nice, Sophie." She swallowed hard. "I found out he slept with Megan." She started crying.

I said, "You okay?"

"I didn't even like him that much. I don't know. I can't believe Megan."

"It was probably just as much his fault." I tried to defend Megan a little, not because I like her but just because I feel so guilty.

Abi wiped her eyes. "I have other stuff to deal with. I don't think Megan was very good for me anyway. She . . ." She swallowed again. "She started the whole throwing-up thing." She paused. "I'm going to see my doctor tomorrow."

I didn't reply, but I was glad because I realized that Abi wanting help is a big step. Abi chatting to me as we walked through the crowded hallways kind of felt like old times. And kind of not. I'm not sure we'll ever be like we were. I don't think I mind as much as I did, though. I hope she gets better.

I hope I do.

197

After I finished my homework tonight, I was lying in my room. Mum came in with a rucksack—the rucksack Emily brought home that day last summer, the day before she died. I sat up and looked at Mum. She pulled out some brittle twigs, and it took me a moment to remember they were for Em's family tree project.

I looked at Mum for what felt like ages but was probably only about two seconds.

She said, "There's a memorial service. They've asked me to say something. I want to make this and I want you to help." It sounded rehearsed.

I realized how hard she was trying—how hard she had tried. And I knew it was time for me to try a little harder, too. I said, with a little break in my voice, "Help how?"

"I thought we could make something together."

I paused for a long moment.

She looked down; I could see the hope leaking out of her.

I looked at the brittle twigs she'd laid out. I said, "How do we make it?"

She caught my eye and smiled. "I don't know. Maybe we should do it differently. We could make it represent her in some way. I don't know how, though."

I wanted to cry then, really badly, but I swallowed down the tears. I said, "We could make a tree with the twigs, then color in paper leaves and write on them to say what she was like."

Mum nodded.

We started at the bottom and worked our way to the top, leaf by leaf. It wasn't as beautiful as the tree Emily could have made, it probably wasn't as artistic, but it was colorful.

"Emily would have liked this," Mum said, hanging a purple leaf on one side of the tree. "This could be *Generous*."

"We need a leaf for *Funny*. She was funny."

She paused for a second, and then she nodded.

I colored some leaves in bright orange. I lifted one and said, "I want this one to be a memory I have of Emily holding my hand on the beach in Greece once."

She nodded.

All I could think to say was, "I miss her."

Mum started to cry; the tears just fell out of her. She said, "I miss her all the time. Every time I take a breath, I think about her. How could I not? But that doesn't mean I don't think about you and what you've been through, Sophie. What you've seen. I wish I could take it away to make it better for you. But I can't. I can't undo what happened. And I can't undo the state I was in. I'm so sorry." She looked at me, and I saw her eyes were flecked with gold. I'd never noticed before. "But you have to know this, Sophie. I don't *ever* wish it was you instead. I never once wished that."

I said, "I know. I always felt like she was your favorite." And then because I couldn't say anything else, I was so choked up, I turned to write on an orange leaf.

She said, "I love you both the same. I always have. And just imagine, that day of the bombing, it could have been both of you. It doesn't bear thinking about how awful it would be if I lost you, my littlest daughter." She wiped her eyes. Then she cut out a large leaf and said, "This one could be us: we were part of her life. Me, you, and your father."

"Yeah . . . Dad." I held my breath. "Mum, about Robin. I'm trying to be nice, but it's taking me a while to get used to him being around. I've found it difficult. . . ."

"Robin is just supportive of me right now. He's a good friend, that's all. I'm still too sad for anything more."

"I feel sad all the time. And I have panic attacks. They make me feel like I'm dying. Was that what it was like for her, do you think? Dying, I mean."

"Oh, Sophie."

"I think about it constantly. The blood, the screaming, the panic, the flames."

She nodded and took my hand.

I looked up at her. "Your eyes have changed color," I said. "They've got golden bits in."

"Really?" she said. And then we sat there for a while, her fingers laced in mine.

THURSDAY, JUNE 29TH

After school today Rosa-Leigh, Kalila, and I went shopping for summer clothes. Kalila's amazing at finding bargains. We got some great stuff.

FRIDAY, JUNE 30TH

We had a talk at school about exams and our future. Maybe I'll be a doctor. No, I don't think I could cope with all the blood. Maybe I'd like to be a counselor, or a psychiatrist, or psychologist, someone who helps people. I might be good at that. I'll have to work harder on listening to other people. And I'll have to do better at school. I haven't got very good marks this year, although I've finally started working harder, because I'm worried about next year. I have loads of catching up to do.

I got home, did some homework, and sat watching TV in a pool of sunshine. A bird flew into the window of our house with a loud knock. I ran outside. A poor little sparrow lay on the grass panting and panicking. I crouched and held my hands around it. It twitched and fluttered in a panic, but I wanted to save it from Fluffy, who was prowling round. After a while it perked up and took a couple of steps. It flew off.

After that I went to find Mum. I blurted out, "Can we go to see her grave?"

"You want to? When I asked you before, you didn't want to come with me."

I nodded. "I want to."

She tugged her car keys out of her pocket. "Let's go, then."

The graveyard at the church in Highgate is quiet. The graves are in higgledy-piggledy lines, and in the sunlight the cemetery is a beautiful place. Emily's grave is over by a line of trees. We sat next to it. I read her name, her age, looked at the flowers someone had left. Nothing happened, and I didn't feel good or bad. I just enjoyed Emily, Mum, and me sitting there all together—even though Emily wasn't there, she *was*, if that makes any sense—and time went by.

THURSDAY, JULY 6TH

It's the memorial service tomorrow.

FRIDAY, JULY 7TH

We balanced Emily's tree in the back of the car next to me and drove to the memorial service. Well, Robin drove.

Once we arrived, I began to feel light-headed. There were loads of people standing around. We waited for a bit, and Mum went to put Emily's tree by the stage area. Then this old woman went up and spoke into the microphone. She started by reading all the names of the people who'd died in the bombing. When she read out Emily's name, I thought I might collapse. Then I saw a tall guy I recognized. It came back to me immediately: he was the guy who'd helped me out of the tunnel. He had a scar along one cheek, running under one eye. He was holding a single red rose.

Another guy came over to us. Simon. Emily's boyfriend, at art college. I'd met him at her funeral. Mum leaned over and said, "Hi. Nice to see you, Simon." And then, "Thank you for coming."

Simon said, "We all miss her," and he gestured over to a group of people. Emily's friends from art college. Some of them were crying. Her whole other life. And a familiar anger rose from my stomach, but then, instead of getting stuck in my throat, it flew out the top of me into the vast open sky. I let out a slow breath. My hands had been clenched, I noticed, so I relaxed them and spread my fingers wide. I smiled over at Emily's friends, and two or three of them must have recognized me from my visits, because they smiled back.

Up on the podium people talked of terrorism and of the suicide bombers who'd made the trains and the bus blow up. I didn't want to hear about them. I didn't want to think about why they'd done what they'd done, because no matter how much I think about it, it never makes any sense or any difference, and it doesn't make me any less angry or sick. Then the politicians stopped speaking and, one by one, people got up to talk about those who'd died. I stood near the stage listening.

Then it was Mum's turn. She stood in front of all these strangers and some of our oldest family friends. The Haywoods were bunched together, Katherine holding Mark tightly. Lucy smiled over at me. Mrs. Haynes and Ms. Bloxam were with a group of other teachers from my school, and witchy Mrs. Haynes nodded over at me with tears in her eyes. Next to them stood Rosa-Leigh and her huge family, with Kalila. Rosa-Leigh waved, and so did Joshua, her oldest brother. A little farther off Abigail huddled with Zara. I smiled at her, then turned back to Mum standing all alone.

Mum seemed like she was about to say something, but then the words must have become stuck, because she gestured at Emily's tree and started crying. I don't know what came over me. I saw her standing there all by herself, and I pushed past the people in front of me and walked up to stand next to her. I said, "It's hard sometimes without Emily for Mum and me to remember we've still got each other." I slipped my hand in hers and she squeezed hard.

And then we both took it in turns to talk to all those people about my sister. It probably wasn't the best speech in the world. But it felt to me like it was. And at the end I said, "I want to add one thing."

My heart pounded, but I made myself read out this poem. I added a verse to the end; I think it's better now.

> *"The sticks on the trees*
> *Stand up harsh and bare*
> *With rings on their fingers*
> *And knots in their hair*
>
> *"The silver of winter*
> *Is smoky with rain*
> *The witches of sunlight*
> *Fly low again*
>
> *"In a puddle of grey*
> *Last summer lies*
> *Where nothing can swim*
> *And my sister dies*
>
> *"The spring is weighted*
> *With what has been*
> *And she's still with me*
> *Brightly unseen."*

I looked out at the crowd. Some of the people had tears on their cheeks or tissues pressed against their faces. Then I looked at Mum. She was staring at me, her eyes shining like bubbles blown by a child.

WEDNESDAY, JULY 12TH

After school I went to see Koreen, the other therapist. I told her that, to help me, Lynda had given me a book to write in and that I've nearly filled every page. Koreen said she'd get me a new book so I could carry on. I thanked her but said I could buy my own.

We talked more about panic attacks, about Emily, and the memorial service, about my mum. And then I started talking about the bombing and what it was like that day. Just talking about it made me panic, but Koreen listened and waited while I got through. I realized it's okay that it's going to take me a long time to recover after what's happened. It's normal.

SUNDAY, JULY 16TH

At Sunday lunch, which Mum spent ALL morning preparing, she and I were bickering because she wanted me to carve the chicken but I thought she should do it. Robin gazed at the ceiling—obviously pretending not to be in the room.

Mum suddenly said, mid-bicker, "I've bought you and me a flight to Italy this summer. We'll go for two weeks." That shut me up.

Robin's not invited, and he doesn't seem to mind at all.

He said, "It's important you and your mum spend time together."

I kind of felt fond of him for about two whole minutes. Then he started telling a really long story about some trip he took in Bolivia five years ago, and I almost passed out with boredom.

MONDAY, JULY 17TH

Rosa-Leigh told me at lunch today that she's having an end-of-school party for both our birthdays at her amazing house. She's already organized everything.

THURSDAY, JULY 20TH

LAST DAY OF SCHOOL. Rosa-Leigh called to chat about her party. When I got off the phone, I sat around in the kitchen with Mum and Robin. Mum said she was going to Boxercise, so I ended up going with her again. I think I'll go every week.

FRIDAY, JULY 21ST

Robin bought me a great dress for the party. It fits perfectly. It's turquoise and silky and gorgeous, and I can't believe he chose so well.

I woke up when it was REALLY EARLY and still dark. I climbed onto the roof. The air had a summery feel, and I thought of the time Emily and I had sat up there and waited for sunrise. I started working on a found poem. I used words from the pages I'd written in this notebook, which isn't technically a found poem. I might show the poem to Mum.

Emily

> *The windows failed*
> *I could not see*
>   *to see*

> *Hold on to her tightly*

> *She's generous*
>   *(an orange leaf)*

> *Hugeness shut quietly*
> *I suddenly couldn't breathe*
>   *(take deep breaths)*
> *If only*
> *I could go back*
>   *if only it would make sense*

> *I held her hand*
>> *watched the sun go down*
> *Briefly*

When I was finished, I looked up and light streaked the sky in fingers of pink and blue. Then, as I was watching, the sun glimmered over the roofs of the houses and appeared in a fireball of molten orange. I blinked. For a moment I could have sworn Emily was sitting right there next to me.

MONDAY, JULY 24TH

I went out today and bought a new book for when this one runs out, which it's about to. The new book's got a map of the world on the front cover.

FRIDAY, JULY 28TH

Kalila and I are going to the party together. Can't wait! Rosa-Leigh's brother Joshua is going to be there, and I know this for a FACT because he TOLD Rosa-Leigh to tell me he would be. She says if I really like him then she doesn't mind, but I don't know! I like him, I think, but I don't know if I even want to get involved with anyone right now. Oh, I don't know.

I'm wearing the silky dress Robin got me, which feels

fantastic against my skin. Emily would love this dress. I'd let her borrow it if she were still here. It feels like she is sometimes. Those times are good.

I have to get ready. Kalila will be here in a minute.

ACKNOWLEDGMENTS

Thank you, Lynne, Susan, and Sarah S, for pushing this novel to be what it is now.

Thanks, Kelley Jo Burke and the Saskatchewan Arts Board, for supporting me.

Thank you, Jackie and Natasha, for everything you've done for me and for my books.

Thank you, Ellie, Ellen, Jenny, Dad, and Anneke, for reading early drafts.

Thanks, Leona and Jill, for the lunches and writerly conversation.

Thank you, Juliette, just because.

And thank you, Yann, for it all.